TOUCHED BY TWO WARS

France, 1914: Isabelle and her mother are pleased to take in British soldiers as they pass through the countryside on their way to the front. But Isabelle's attempt to comfort a distressed soldier leaves her with an illegitimate yet dearly beloved daughter, Madeleine. As Isabelle and her own mother struggle with the upkeep of Château Bellevais, another soldier, James, comes into her life — and out again. During the ensuing chaos of yet another war, Isabelle flees to England. Is it possible that she and James could find each other once more?

DAWN KNOX

---◆---

TOUCHED BY TWO WARS

Complete and Unabridged

LINFORD
Leicester

First published in Great Britain in 2018

First Linford Edition
published 2020

Northamptonshire
Libraries

A catalogue record for this book is available
from the British Library.

ISBN 978–1–4448–4429–0

Published by
Ulverscroft Limited
Anstey, Leicestershire

Set by Words & Graphics Ltd.
Anstey, Leicestershire
Printed and bound in Great Britain by
T. J. International Ltd., Padstow, Cornwall

This book is printed on acid-free paper

1

1917

Hélène Rousseau hardly dared breathe for fear of waking the tiny, exhausted baby in her arms. A rush of emotion coursed through her — overwhelming love, a crushing fear of the future and the steadfast determination to protect her granddaughter with her life.

The delivery had been long and gruelling for mother and baby and there had been times when Hélène feared she might lose one, or perhaps both. But at last, the tiny scrap of humanity had emerged and although her cry had not been as strong as it might have been, Hélène thought it had spirit, and that her granddaughter was claiming her place in the world.

All fanciful nonsense of course, but this child would need courage to cope with what was to come. After all, there was only so much a grandmother and mother could do . . .

Madame Grimaud plumped up the pillows and did her best to rearrange the crumpled sheets around the exhausted mother as Hélène sat on the edge of the bed and held the sleeping baby.

'See, Isabelle, she's perfect!'

'Oh, Maman! I can't believe it. She's so beautiful!'

Madame Grimaud snorted. 'She's going to need a lot more than good looks, if you ask me!'

Hélène fished in her pocket and withdrew several coins, 'Thank you for your help, Madame. Isabelle and I are very grateful to you.' She stood, ready to escort the midwife from her daughter's bedroom, but Madame Grimaud was in no hurry.

'Well, even though I say so myself, I did a good job. Without my skills, she'd probably have died. Although when she's old enough to know better, she might not thank you. It might've been kinder for the poor little mite if she hadn't lived. Such a burden she'll have to bear.'

'Thank you, Madame, I'm sure we'll manage. Well, I think that will be all,' Hélène said, holding out her arms to usher the midwife out.

Madame Grimaud turned over the coins in her palm and raised her eyes expectantly.

'Of course,' she added in confidential tones, 'you and Mademoiselle Rousseau can rely on my continuing . . . er . . . discretion.'

With a sigh, Hélène placed two more Francs on the outstretched palm and after a brief inspection, Madame Grimaud snapped her fingers tightly over them. Conveying the coins to her bag, she dropped them into its depths.

Continuing discretion . . . what did that mean? Absolutely nothing because everyone in the small town knew that Hélène's unmarried daughter had been expecting a child. Montplessis was a small, rural community which had not changed its narrow-minded attitudes for years. Despite its proximity to Paris, it shared none of the capital city's cosmopolitan views and the inhabitants had been scandalised by what they considered Isabelle's brazen behaviour. The identity of the father had been discussed in the bar, shops, church, and as was so often pointed out, it could have been any one of hundreds of men.

Hélène knew who the father was, but as far as she was concerned, it didn't really matter. He was now long gone and was unlikely to ever be aware of his new daughter.

2

1914

Looking back on it, Isabelle's expectations that her sixteenth birthday would be the start of something important, proved to be remarkably accurate. However, she'd assumed that any changes would take place in her — she hoped she would feel more grown up and then Maman and Papa would take her more seriously.

She knew, of course, that there would be no party in the family château in Montplessis until she reached twenty-one, but she hoped she would be allowed a few friends for tea and she was almost certain Maman would ask Cook to bake a cake.

However, the innocent celebrations she'd hoped for never came to pass because on the third of August, 1914, the day before her birthday, France and Germany declared war against each other. The transition to adulthood took place with shocking speed when a few months later, her father, Philippe Rousseau, who'd left home to defend his country, was killed on the battlefield, leaving Isabelle and her mother broken-hearted and alone.

Without the constant attention of Philippe, the old château began to fall into disrepair. Once an elegant building which had been in the Rousseau family for generations, Château Bellevais' glory began to fade as age and weather took its toll.

Window shutters hung at varying angles as they dangled from one hinge, paint peeled from wood, and on the roof, tiles had been dislodged during a particularly savage storm and had slithered to the neglected garden below. Overcome with grief, Hélène lost interest in the château and closed many of the rooms, surrendering them to dust and cobwebs. Only two bedrooms, the kitchen and a sitting room were still used.

Cook had gone to live with her sister in Brittany and the gardener and farmhands had joined up at the same time as Philippe. The gardener had been seriously wounded and would never tend a garden again. There had been no news of the labourers for weeks.

Hélène refused to believe that the Germans would advance so far into France that she and Isabelle would be forced to flee or to live under occupation — but then no one would have believed the Germans could have advanced as far as they had into Belgium and France.

It was the arrival of the British troops in 1914 that gave them hope — and changed their lives.

Hélène and Isabelle had been pleased to take in British soldiers as they passed through the countryside on their way to the Front and accommodated large numbers of them in their barn, as well as cleaning out several of the rooms they had previously closed to make them ready for officers. There had been a steady stream of men arriving fresh from England — some no more than boys — with faces that betrayed eagerness and optimism as they headed for the trenches.

After spending time in the frontline and reserve trenches, soldiers returned to Montplessis to rest, though as Isabelle discovered there was very little 'rest'. The soldiers were kept busy with drills, weapon cleaning and training but they always seemed to have energy for a game of football.

Many helped Hélène to carry out maintenance on the château, mending the window shutters and guttering, and replacing roof tiles.

If it hadn't been for the endless stream of wounded being tended in the dressing station that had been set up in Montplessis, the sound of artillery which drifted on the breeze, and the deep ache at losing her father, Isabelle might have been content. There was always someone to talk to and usually a willing pair of hands ready to help if the work in the garden was heavy.

Her English, which had been good before the outbreak of war, improved considerably. Hélène had learned to speak English when she'd stayed with her elder brother, Henri, and his English wife in Guildford. Once married and settled in France, Hélène had no further opportunity to practise although she'd taught a rather reluctant Isabelle. But now with so many British soldiers passing through, their command of the language increased and they were even able to distinguish various British accents.

By June 1916, life in the château had settled into a rhythm. Not normality exactly, but there was a pattern to their lives. Earlier hopes that the fighting would be over by the first Christmas — and then the second — proved unfounded. When news came from Britain that conscription had been introduced, Isabelle began to wonder what would happen when there were no more men of fighting age left.

In June, there was a change in the mood of the soldiers. It had first been noticeable among the senior officers but gradually, it filtered down through the ranks. No one spoke about what was causing such great anticipation and excitement in front of Isabelle, and she began to wonder if perhaps the British army knew it was winning. There was a great deal of frenetic activity as large numbers of troops, horses and artillery passed through the countryside, heading towards the River Somme. Perhaps this was the final effort before they won the war.

On the twenty-third of June, there were thunderstorms and the following day brought low cloud and more heavy rain. At six in the morning, Isabelle thought more storms were approaching until she realised the terrific noise wasn't thunder but was the sound of shells and bombs exploding.

It all made sense now. The snatches of overheard conversation and the massive movement of men, horses and equipment towards the Somme. She'd heard whispers of 'the big push', and guessed the Tommies were attacking the German strongholds.

The previous day, she'd watched their current 'guests' leave for the front. Captain Western and Lieutenant Marshall had been staying in the château while their men were billeted in the barn and she had been more touched by them than the countless officers who had already passed through their home. The British Army's regulation that men should wear a moustache seemed not so much to confer manliness to the two young officers, who were only a few years older than Isabelle, but rather to highlight their immaturity and inexperience. It would be some time before the down on their top lips would become whiskery and lend the intended air of authority, Isabelle thought. Although as they marched away to fight, she knew their chance of ever achieving a respectable moustache was now slight.

The two shy and reserved officers had been so mindful that Hélène and Isabelle might consider their presence an imposition, they'd created an atmosphere of awkwardness with their meticulous manners and formal politeness which had only eased slightly when Hélène had insisted they make themselves at home.

'Please, gentlemen, relax! Consider it my pleasure to make you comfortable while you stay with us. It is a privilege to have you here, both in our country fighting for us, and in this château.'

After dinner, the men told Isabelle and Hélène about life in England and although they only allowed themselves one glass of wine each, they became less inhibited as their final evening in the château progressed. Captain Western taught Hélène the notes of *It's A Long Way To Tipperary* on the piano, while Lieutenant Marshall and Isabelle played chess.

Hélène had warned her daughter against getting attached to any of the British soldiers but Isabelle showed no sign of flirting with the young lieutenant — they were simply enjoying the game. With her long, dark hair and heart-shaped face, Isabelle was a beautiful girl but Hélène noted with approval that Lieutenant Marshall was behaving like a perfect English gentleman. It was unlikely that either man would return, assuming they were still alive at the end of whatever plans were being put in place near the River Somme. Hélène was satisfied her daughter was mature enough to resist allowing herself to fall for any of these men.

* * *

The massive bombardment continued for a week. Soldiers who'd been wounded and brought to the dressing station in Montplessis spoke about how they were destroying the German lines

13

and how the British would shortly stroll across No Man's Land and take over the enemy trenches without resistance. Bad weather delayed the attack and it wasn't until the first of July that Isabelle heard the shrill whistles in the distance signalling the men to climb out of their trenches and begin the assault. The hair stood up on the back of her neck as she heard the explosions of mines that had been tunnelled under the Germans and felt the earth tremble. Even the cows she was milking seemed nervous, as if they sensed something momentous was happening.

Such terrible destruction! But if it ended the war and further loss of life, then surely it would be worth it.

However, as the days passed, it became clear from the large numbers of wounded who flooded into the dressing station in Montplessis and passed from there to various military hospitals, that things had not gone according to plan. The ferocious bombardment which was thought to have driven the Germans out of their trenches had failed. Many of the enemy had been hiding in fortified, underground bunkers during the artillery fire and as soon as the Allies attacked, the Germans climbed out of their shelters and killed and wounded thousands of Allied soldiers as they walked across No Man's Land.

Hélène agreed to allow men who had minor injuries or who were recuperating, to stay in the château and there was little time to do anything other than care for them. Gradually the numbers of wounded men decreased slightly and word came from the Front that both sides had dug in. The war appeared to be no closer to ending.

Isabelle and Hélène joined the other townspeople in helping the war effort, providing food, sheets to be cut into bandages, and anything else they had which could assist the seemingly endless torrent of wounded men.

Two weeks after the first wave of attacks, Isabelle decided to see if she could help the nurses in the dressing station. Rain was lashing down, so there wasn't much she could do in the garden. Hélène was preparing soup for the soldiers and Isabelle promised to return later to help her mother carry the pot to the dressing station. She pulled her coat over her head and picked her way through the muddy puddles created by the constant movement of boots, hooves and cartwheels along the single road through Montplessis.

At the church, she stepped back out of the way of a bedraggled troop of men who were returning from the Front and waited for them to pass. They were obviously exhausted and Isabelle remembered when the men had marched with energetic strides to what they had assumed would be victory. Now, they seemed oblivious to the rain that dripped off their helmets, heads drooping, eyes downcast and backs stooped under the weight of heavy packs.

'Miss,' said one of the soldiers,

raising his hand in salute, and others then noticed her waiting for them to pass and greeted her too.

She suddenly realised these were men whose officers were Captain Western and Lieutenant Marshall. She rushed to the front where one man was leading the platoon. He was limping and she could see from his face that he was in pain, but he walked with his shoulders back as if pretending that all was well.

She gasped when she realised it was Lieutenant Marshall. The last time she'd seen him, he'd been a young man full of patriotic enthusiasm, leading his troops to certain victory. Now his face was haggard and his eyes held the haunted look of a man who had seen indescribable horrors.

Isabelle's request to the quartermaster had resulted in Lieutenant Marshall lodging in Château Bellevais, and his troops in the barn. She had enquired about Captain Western but he and many of his men had apparently been killed during the first wave of attacks.

Dinner in the château that evening was a sombre affair. Hélène, Isabelle and Lieutenant Marshall were lost in their own memories of the last time they'd been together with Captain Western. Anyway, what was there to talk about?

Lieutenant Marshall pointedly avoided relating any of his recent experiences at the Front, and Hélène and her daughter did not want to remind him. The war had touched every part of their lives and it was hard to recall what life had been like before. Topics that had once been considered suitable to discuss during dinner, now seemed trivial and irrelevant.

Hélène had not expected a guest and had only saved enough soup for her and Isabelle from the batch she'd made earlier for the soldiers in the dressing station. She watered down two portions for herself and her daughter, and gave Lieutenant Marshall the largest share. Apparently, he hadn't eaten for twenty-four hours and the two women were happy to ensure he didn't go to bed hungry.

Hélène opened a bottle of Philippe's best red wine. What was the point of storing up the best of anything when life was so fragile? It was good to enjoy things while you could. Neither Philippe nor Captain Western would take pleasure in vintage wine again.

After dinner, she led them into the drawing room and poured them all a glass of cognac. There was only a drop left, but who knew if or when there would ever be anything to celebrate again?

'Please help yourself when you return, Lieutenant. If you think you may need some help sleeping,' Hélène said when he announced he was going to check on his men. 'I wouldn't normally encourage drinking but I've heard stories from some of the men in the dressing station and if half of them are true, you and your men have been through a most traumatic time.'

Isabelle followed her mother up the sweeping staircase to bed. Her stomach rumbled and she wished there had been more food at dinner but Lieutenant Marshall had needed it. She wondered if she should have drunk quite so much wine and cognac on an empty stomach, as her legs felt as if they had a life of their own. Still, once she was in bed, she could sleep it off, and early tomorrow she'd search for eggs. If she was lucky, she'd be able to make them all omelettes for breakfast.

⋆   ⋆   ⋆

Isabelle woke some time later from a deep sleep. There were noises coming from downstairs and it took her a few seconds to realise it was probably the lieutenant returning from the barn. A door banged and there was a clatter, followed by an exclamation. Isabelle lit a candle and checked the time. It was just after one o'clock and she wondered if the fire had burned down so low that the lieutenant, who wasn't familiar with the layout of the château, couldn't see where to go.

She wrapped a shawl round her nightgown and, taking the candle, she tiptoed downstairs. The lieutenant was sitting in Hélène's chair in the drawing room, in front of the fire, with elbows on his knees, staring at the dying embers.

'I'm so sorry to have woken you, Made moiselle,' he said when he saw her. 'I apologise for the noise. I tripped over the footstool — I'm afraid I'm not too steady on my feet. The boys insisted I share their rum and the time slipped away. Please, go back to bed.'

He placed his hands on the arms of the chair and pushed himself up, but as he turned, he staggered and she stepped forward to hold his arm. 'Allow me to help you, Lieutenant.'

'Tom, my name's Tom.' He lurched sideways and she held on to him more firmly.

'Well, Tom, I think it's time you went to bed.'

'Yes, I think so . . . ' He sighed. 'But I don't think I'll be able to sleep. Whenever I close my eyes, I see terrible things. I thought I might stay here.'

Remembering the cognac her mother had left, she poured him a glass. 'Maman said you might like this to help you sleep.'

He took the glass and holding it up, he watched the glow of the fire through the amber liquid. 'Perhaps, Mademoiselle, you would drink with me? It would be rude to drink alone.'

'My name's Isabelle.'

She poured herself a drop of cognac and sat next to him on the sofa. He was several years older than her and had so much more experience of life, but she knew the alcohol had impaired his coordination and blunted his thoughts. For the first time, she felt older and more worldly-wise than him, and although she knew the cognac had affected her too, she had more control over her faculties. She felt like an adult distracting a distraught child. 'Tell me what it was like growing up in England, Tom.'

If he suspected she was trying to divert his attention from his recent experiences, he gave no sign, and spoke enthusiastically about his childhood dream of becoming an engineer. He told her about life with his parents and brother in London and how he'd loved making things and taking things apart.

She described what growing up in the French countryside had been like and her excitement when she'd been taken on trips to Paris.

As the fire died down and they shared reminiscences, the world and its problems receded, creating a special atmosphere that wrapped them up and bound them together. The recognition that it was a temporary state which would be broken as soon as one of them returned to real life also retreated as they talked and moved closer together under the blanket that Isabelle had put over them.

The illusion that she had been in control of the situation faltered slightly when he placed his forehead against hers and held her face in his hands. A strange feeling in the pit of her stomach started to radiate throughout her body, thrilling her in a way that she'd never experienced before.

When his lips touched hers, she held her breath. Common sense was telling her to pull away, but her body told her to press closer, to give herself up to the pleasure washing over her.

★   ★   ★

It seemed that she'd only just closed her eyes when a bird started its song and she knew morning had arrived. Isabelle was shocked at the sensation of Tom's bare skin against hers and her cheeks burned with embarrassment. It was tempting to slip out of his embrace, dress and leave him to wake on his own, but if Maman came down

— which she would soon — she'd find him naked under the blanket. She put her nightgown back on and gently shook his shoulder.

'Tom, wake up.'

He opened his eyes slowly and groaned.

'Mademoiselle?' He looked about as if he didn't know where he was.

As he sat up, the blanket moved and he clutched at it, realising his nakedness.

'Isabelle,' she said in alarm, 'I'm Isabelle.' She'd expected the bubble to burst when the morning came but after sharing something so intimate, he surely hadn't forgotten her name?

His eyes now moved rapidly back and forth as if he was re-running the night's events.

'What've I done?' he looked aghast. 'I . . . I'm so sorry!' He held his head in his hands.

She shook her head in disbelief. The closeness that had bound them was gone. How could he be sorry? Hadn't they clung to each other in ecstasy a short while ago? Hadn't she kissed away his tears and tried to erase his pain?

Isabelle turned away to hide her brimming eyes.

'I'll leave you to dress,' she said in the most business-like voice she could manage.

★ ★ ★

By the time she returned from feeding the chickens and animals, Hélène was making breakfast. The cushions on the sofa in the drawing room where she and Tom had shared each other's bodies were plumped up, although she knew her mother hadn't done it because they were not in the same positions as usual. She tried not to draw attention to herself as she rearranged them and put the folded blanket back in the cupboard. It looked as though no one had sat on the sofa, let alone slept the night there.

'Will you call Lieutenant Marshall

please, Chérie? Breakfast is ready.'

Isabelle was summoning the courage to face him when there was a knock on the front door.

'Mornin', Miss. Private Newman, Miss.' It was one of Tom's men. 'Err, if you don't mind. I've come to collect Lieutenant Marshall's things. I'm sorry to bother you. It won't take a second . . . '

She stood back to allow him in. He hesitated, his ruddy cheeks deepening in colour. 'Err, if you wouldn't mind showing me to his room, Miss . . . '

'Yes, yes, of course.' She led him upstairs. 'Will the lieutenant be staying in the barn?' She asked as casually as she could.

'Oh no, Miss, he's volunteered for a special operation. I can't say more than that, I'm afraid.'

'Will it be . . . ?' she hesitated. Well of course it would be dangerous — what a stupid thing to ask!

'Dangerous, Miss? Sounds like sui-cide to me. He's a brave bloke, you've

27

got to give 'im that.'

Private Newman gathered up Tom's belongings and hurried downstairs.

'Lieutenant Marshall left early this morning on a special operation, Maman, so he won't be needing breakfast.'

Disappointment and relief jostled with each other. She wouldn't have to face him and risk her mother noticing that something had changed, but then neither would she have the opportunity to ask him if what they'd done had been so terrible. She wondered if he would have volunteered for such a hazardous mission had they not spent the night together. She'd wanted to comfort him — not send him to almost certain death.

'Are you all right, Chérie? You seem a bit tired, not quite yourself.'

'I didn't sleep well, Maman, but I'm fine.'

'If you want a bit of fresh air later, you could ride over to Beauvais and see when the photographs will be ready.'

'Photographs?'

'Oh, yes, I forgot to tell you, Lieutenant Marshall asked me yesterday if I would keep his ticket and pick up his photographs. He gave me the money and his address in England so that . . . well, if anything happens to him, I could post them home. Apparently, when the men arrived back from the Front, many of them had their photographs taken in a studio in Beauvais so they had something to send home to their families.'

'Yes, of course, Maman.'

It would be a relief to get out of the château and Isabelle was intrigued by the thought of seeing Tom's photograph. Papa had also visited the studio in Beauvais and a framed sepia photograph of him in his uniform stood on the mantelpiece in the drawing room — watching over what had taken place on the sofa last night, she realised with shame.

★   ★   ★

There was a queue of British soldiers outside the studio waiting to have their photographs taken and it took some time before the photographer's assistant was able to tell her that Lieutenant Marshall's pictures were ready. Isabelle paid and placed the envelope carefully in her bag.

'Hello, darlin'! Come and 'ave a photograph taken with me!' one of the privates in the queue called out and others joined in good-naturedly, calling for her to pose with them.

She smiled and waved, wishing them good luck. They were obviously new recruits, young and full of optimism — like all those who'd passed through Montplessis not so long ago.

When she got home, she showed Hélène the photographs. Tom was standing in front of a blank background, his arm resting on the back of a chair and he seemed relaxed and composed.

'A handsome man,' said Hélène. 'We'll hold on to them for a few days in case he . . . ' she paused and then continued, 'For when he gets back. I'm sure he'd like to see them and write a message on the back.'

Isabelle slipped the photographs in the envelope and when Hélène turned away, she put them in her pocket, went upstairs to her bedroom and hid them in her underwear drawer.

★ ★ ★

Men continued to pour into Montplessis on their way to the British lines and many — too many — returned shortly after in ambulances on their way to the dressing station or to one of the military hospitals. Isabelle made enquiries about Tom but no one knew where he was, or if they did, they didn't tell her.

By mid-October, she was beginning to despair. Conditions at the Front had deteriorated with the unseasonal rains and many of the men returned from their time in the trenches with Trench

Foot as a result of standing in water for days, as well as suffering from dysentery and other illnesses from the unsanitary conditions. The cold and wet was affecting Isabelle too. She felt drained of energy and alarmingly, for the last two weeks, she'd been sick — the sight of breakfast which was usually so welcome, making her heave and rush from the kitchen.

One morning, Hélène cleared the table and asked Isabelle to sit down. She sighed and looked sadly at her daughter.

'I'm all right, Maman. I just have a stomach upset. Don't worry it'll be gone soon,' she said, misreading her mother's serious expression.

'Chérie,' Hélène said shaking her head and placing her hand on top of Isabelle's. She looked at her daughter's swollen stomach. 'I'm afraid I have to ask . . . and please be honest with me for I fear what you have will not be gone soon, and if I'm right, it will drastically change both our lives.'

3

1918

'Hello, Miss! You're the girl who lives in the château, aren't you?'

Isabelle studied the sergeant's face. She'd met so many soldiers during the last four years that it was hard to remember them all.

'Sergeant Newman,' he said. 'I was Private Newman when I was here last. Me an' me mates billeted in your barn in 1916.'

'Oh, yes, I remember. How are you, Sergeant?'

'Really happy now, Miss! I've got a Blighty One. I'll be off home shortly.' He nodded at his right arm. What was left of it was strapped in a sling. 'I can't do anything for the war effort with a dodgy arm, so they're sending me back to Blighty.'

Isabelle suspected he wouldn't be able to do anything ever again with his dodgy arm, but he seemed happy to have what the British soldiers called a 'Blighty One' — orders to be sent home following a wound that stopped a man being any further use to the army.

'Just a shame I didn't get it earlier. I've missed four years of me son's life . . . ' He shook his head sadly. 'The little nipper was born just before I joined up. Still, I'll be home by the end of the week. If I hadn't been shot so bad, I'd have been patched up and sent back to the Front,' he said, nodding his head at the soldiers around him in the dressing station. 'Most of this lot will be on their way back to the trenches in a few days. But I'm one of the lucky ones. Most of the men in the platoon who stayed in your barn are dead.'

'Did anyone hear what happened to Lieutenant Marshall?' Isabelle asked as casually as she could. Her heart was thumping in her chest.

'Yeah, lucky sod! He got a Blighty

One a couple o' months ago. Oh, beggin' your pardon for the language, Miss.'

'So he's still alive?'

'As far as I know. 'E did a lot of special ops — but against all odds, he survived. 'E'll be back at home with his wife by now, though. He was a good man. Brave. One o' the bravest. All the men looked up to him.'

'Mademoiselle Rousseau, that man there needs a bed pan, if you please.' It was the sister in charge of the dressing station.

Isabelle was grateful for the opportunity to turn away so Sergeant Newman couldn't see the tears that filled her eyes.

She had been wrong about growing up magically on her sixteenth birthday and suddenly becoming an adult. It had taken her four more years, the birth of her illegitimate daughter, Madeleine, and the knowledge that the man she'd imagined had special feelings for her was married and living in another country. She could now see that the dream of Tom coming back for her and Madeleine was just childish nonsense.

Why hadn't she listened to Maman when she'd tried to explain that even if Tom was alive, he may not be happy to know he had a daughter? The fairytale world she'd spun for herself had shielded her from the contempt of her neighbours when her pregnancy became obvious, because she'd believed that one day Tom would come for her and Madeleine.

Sergeant Newman's news smashed the fairy tale into tiny pieces. She would never see the world in the same way. Now, she was an adult.

★　★　★

When Isabelle arrived home, she was disappointed to see a horse tethered outside the château. She'd been looking forward to seeing her daughter and playing with her before bedtime, but during the evenings when Monsieur

Charbonel called, Madeleine usually became fractious, and Isabelle spent most of the time comforting her, rather than having fun.

For the last few weeks, Monsieur Charbonel had visited regularly, usually arriving unannounced shortly before dinner and appearing reluctant to accept Hélène's invitation to share their meal — although he was easily persuaded. He was sure to send a gift the following day to show his gratitude — usually something that wasn't widely available, such as steak, oranges, or marzipan. At first Hélène hadn't wanted to accept the gifts because she suspected Monsieur Charbonel was involved in the black market, but she salved her conscience by ensuring that she shared them with the soldiers in the dressing station or with any officers lodging at the château.

Strangely, Monsieur Charbonel's visits never occurred at the same time that Hélène had guests and Isabelle assumed that a lot of planning was involved in his seemingly casual house calls. Nevertheless, Isabelle was pleased that at least one person from Montplessis hadn't shunned them after Madeleine was born.

Madame Charbonel had died of consumption at the beginning of the war and her husband made it clear he was looking for a new wife. Hélène was still an attractive woman so it wasn't surprising that he was often to be found in their home. But despite Monsieur Charbonel's obvious interest in her mother, Isabelle knew that it was unlikely that she would agree to marry him. Papa had been the love of her life and Hélène would never settle for second best — however wealthy he might be.

Monsieur Charbonel was pleasant enough for an old man, Isabelle thought. His nut-brown, weather-beaten face was topped by thick grey hair and he must have once been quite handsome, but there was something cold and calculating about him that disturbed Isabelle. And strangely, Madeleine seemed to pick up on it too.

When Isabelle went into the drawing room, her daughter was sitting on Hélène's lap. Monsieur Charbonel sat opposite but rose to greet Isabelle.

'Mama!' squealed Madeleine holding out her arms. Isabelle picked her up and swung her around happily.

'Perhaps you would like to stay to dinner, Monsieur?' Hélène asked.

'Well, I don't wish to intrude, but I have something important I'd like to, er . . . discuss with you, so that would be very kind, thank you.'

'Come Madeleine, let's set the table for Mémé and Monsieur Charbonel, shall we?'

Isabelle took her daughter's hand and led her out of the drawing room. If Monsieur Charbonel was about to propose, it was best that she gave them some privacy. It would be hard enough for Maman to reject him without having an audience.

Minutes passed and still Maman and Monsieur Charbonel remained in the drawing room. Isabelle wondered if she should let them know dinner was ready. Perhaps he was finding it hard to summon the courage to propose and he was rambling. Just as she decided she would tap on the door and find out what was going on, Maman came out, followed by Monsieur Charbonel. Her brows were slightly furrowed and she shot Isabelle a glance that told her she was rather puzzled.

'So, Monsieur, you said you had something important to discuss?' said Hélène once they were seated at the table and dinner was served.

'Ah, yes, Madame, or may I call you Hélène?' He cleared his throat. 'Well, it's like this, Hélène. It's several months since my good lady wife passed away and I'm not a man who likes to live on his own. I want to share my life.' He mopped his forehead with a handkerchief. 'I'm a wealthy man and I could be generous to the right woman. So . . . ' He ran his finger round the inside of his shirt collar. 'Well, it's like this. I have a proposition for your daughter . . . Isabelle, if you would do me the honour of accepting my hand I would pay handsomely for the upkeep of the child. I assume you would want it to live here with your mother? I would also pay for the repair and maintenance of the château. In time, perhaps we could live here but there's no hurry. The late Madame Charbonel and I were not blessed with children, so I have no heir but you are young and I hope that in time, we might have children of our own, Mademoiselle.'

The two women stared at him in horror.

'M-monsieur! I . . . well, I simply had no idea!' said Isabelle.

'Oh, please call me Norbert. Of course, as my wife, you'll regain some of the respect you lost when you had . . . ' he pointed at Madeleine with his fork. 'But if you are not seen with

41

the child, people will forget about her in time. It will be like starting afresh. Wiping the slate clean, as it were.' He paused expectantly.

Hélène placed her hands on the table and slowly rose, her voice calm and dignified.

'You have the nerve to ask my daughter to marry you and also to abandon her daughter, Monsieur! Get out! And don't ever come back!'

'Hélène! I've made her a very fair offer. Who else is going to want her with another man's bastard? I could ensure a way back into society, and the child won't suffer. She'll live here with you . . . or elsewhere if you'd like. Just name it and I'll see if I can make it happen.'

'The child, as you call her, has a name. It is Madeleine and she is my granddaughter. What you are proposing is monstrous, Monsieur! To remove Madeleine from her mother!'

'She would live with you, and your daughter would be able to visit from time to time but — '

'Enough!' said Isabelle rising and standing next to her mother, 'I would not marry you, Monsieur, if you were the last man on earth. I suggest you do as my mother has asked — get out and don't ever come back. I will never hand my daughter over to someone else — not even my mother!'

Hearing the tension in her mother's voice, Madeleine began to cry and Isabelle picked her up and held her close.

'You've made a grave mistake, Mademoiselle! I could have shielded you from scandal, but now I see how brazen and shameless you are. Consider my proposal withdrawn. Good evening.'

Balancing Madeleine on one hip, Isabelle joined her mother at the window, and together, they watched the rapidly diminishing figure of the horse and rider.

'I suspect we haven't heard the last of him,' said Hélène.

Isabelle put one arm round her

mother's shoulders. 'I'm so sorry, Maman.'

★ ★ ★

Everyone was talking about the war finally coming to an end. Not that anyone in Montplessis discussed it with either Hélène or Isabelle when they were queuing in the shops or attending church. Whispers passed behind hands and condemning eyes followed their movements and the only people who treated them with respect were the British soldiers and the staff in the dressing station. Wounded men and those who were treating them had more on their mind than a young girl and her illegitimate daughter, and it was likely that not many of them knew about the child or her circumstances anyway.

It was impossible to know whether Monsieur Charbonel had maliciously started rumours about Isabelle or whether people were more aware of Madeleine now she was no longer a tiny baby hidden inside a shawl. Shopkeepers who'd once been happy to chat to Hélène now served her silently, and sometimes even rudely. She insisted on going to the shops instead of Isabelle — if she was treated so discourteously, how would they behave towards her daughter?

One morning, Isabelle returned from feeding the animals and found her mother seated at the kitchen table with her head in her hands. Several letters lay in front of her.

'Maman! What's wrong?'

Silently, Hélène passed her one of the letters and Isabelle scanned it quickly.

'Oh, Maman, I'm so sorry! What terrible news! Poor Aunt Dorothy. Would you like me to get your writing set out?'

'Yes please, Chérie, I'll reply straight away. These other letters are from Dorothy asking if we'd received her news.'

Isabelle looked at the date on the letter informing Hélène that her brother, Henri, had died of his wounds in France, several weeks before.

'This letter took a long time to reach us.'

'They all took a long time to reach us. I can't imagine how they all caught up with each other, since the postmarks show they were posted a few days apart. The only explanation is that mail to our château is not a priority and it piles up until someone can be bothered to deliver it.'

Isabelle fetched her mother's writing box and placed it on the table.

'It's not fair that you're paying for what I've done, Maman.'

'Hush, Chérie, we have our beautiful Madeleine. Can you imagine life without her?'

'No, of course not, but people seem to have long memories and I can't see them ever accepting us — or worse, accepting Madeleine. What happens when she goes to school? I can't protect her there. Everyone says the war will be over soon, and what will happen to us when the soldiers go home?

'Well, Chérie, Aunt Dorothy might have thrown you a lifeline. She's invited us to go to England and stay with her. She says she's lonely without Henri. Why don't you and Madeleine go?'

'I won't go without you, Maman.'

'I can't go, Chérie, this is the last link I have with your father. So many of my memories are here, I couldn't bear to leave them. This land and château is your inheritance. I know the war is nearly over but there are a lot of desperate people about and if it's empty, I don't think it would be long before someone breaks in and takes all our things or even moves in. I don't know how we'd ever get them out.'

'But I can't go without you!'

'You have to, Isabelle! Think of Madeleine! She deserves better than she'll have here.'

'But how will you cope with everything on your own? The animals, the château . . . ?'

'Once you go, people will start to forget about you and Madeleine. The war will be over soon and I'll find someone to work for me. It's the only sensible thing to do. I'll write to Dorothy and tell her that you and Madeleine will be coming as soon as you can get passage on a ship.'

Isabelle was silent. Life here in Montplessis would be unbearable for Madeleine in a few years' time. Didn't she owe it to her daughter to start a new life in the land of her father?

4

Madeleine took a small strip of red felt and looped it into the shape of a flower. She pinched it between finger and thumb and held it close to the hat Isabelle was decorating.

'It needs a little bit of red, Maman — doesn't it, Aunt Dottery?'

Dorothy Dubois smiled.

'She's right, you know, Isabelle. I think millinery must be in your family's blood. Maddie has your eye for detail.'

Madeleine's face lit up as her mother took it from her tiny fingers and stitched it to the hat she was decorating.

'Perfect, Chérie!'

'When can I help properly, Maman? I'm old enough to be trusted with a needle and scissors.' She brushed her chestnut curls out of her eyes and looked at her mother hopefully.

'Since you're so keen, why not look through the box and practise on the left-over bits of trim?'

Isabelle and Dorothy exchanged glances over the head of the tiny girl who needed no further invitation to rummage in the previously out-of-bounds scraps box.

'When you've made something good enough, darling,' said Dorothy, 'I've a very ordinary hat that needs a little bit of magic.'

'Will you really let me put it on a hat, Aunt Dottery?' Madeleine asked, hopping from one foot to the other.

'Yes, darling, but it must be your best work.'

'Oh, yes!'

Madeleine turned back to the box and pulled out some pastel pink tulle. Threading her needle with cotton of the same shade, she carefully pleated it and added some silver sequins. She was

50

determined to practise until she was as good as Maman. Perhaps Aunt Dorothy was right and it did run in her blood. After all, she and Maman had only arrived in England five years ago when she was about a year old and Maman had never decorated a hat before that. And now ladies came to Guildford from London to Aunt Dorothy's dress shop. Not only for the lovely dresses she made on her sewing machine but for the beautiful matching hats Maman made.

One day, they would come from London to buy her hats. She'd been told off at school last week because when she should have been painting a picture of a boat sailing on the ocean, she'd painted a wonderful hat with a large, curling feather and dangling ribbons. Miss Lawson had told her to do as she was told and had torn the painting up but it hadn't mattered because when Madeleine came home from school, she'd drawn the same hat and coloured it with her pencils. And that had led to another idea for a hat . . .

★   ★   ★

Madeleine's curls fell over her face as she concentrated on creating a work of art but Isabelle could picture her daughter's determined expression; her lips would be pressed tightly together and her brows pulled together in concentration. The red felt loops she had fashioned earlier had been simple but effective and Isabelle had been as impressed as she knew Dorothy had been. Since they arrived in Guildford a few days before the war ended, Madeleine spent most of her time with the two women.

Before the war, Henri had worked in a department store in Guildford. Dorothy had designed and made dresses at home which he'd shown to his manager who bought several for the store and promised to consider more. When France and Germany declared war, Henri had been one of the first to volunteer and he was followed shortly after by most of the male employees, including his manager. Dorothy had taken more dresses to the store but the woman who now ran the lady's department had not wanted to take a chance on an 'unknown', as she called Dorothy.

With so many men going off to fight, several businesses closed down and many For Sale signs appeared along the High Street. Dorothy found a shop with a spacious apartment above it in the less fashionable part of Guildford and set about renovating them. When Henri returned, they would run Maison Dubois together — with her flair for dressmaking and his ability as a salesman.

However, life had given Dorothy a gift with one hand but robbed her with the other.

Isabelle sighed — she may only be twenty-five years old but she knew that was how the universe worked — you won something and then you lost something even greater.

When she arrived in England, Isabelle decided to put Lieutenant Tom Marshall out of her mind. That hadn't been easy, knowing his last address was Wimbledon, not a great distance from Guildford. At Dorothy's suggestion, she had taken Tom's name, albeit a French version, and her aunt had introduced her as Madame Maréchal saying that her husband had died during the war. Isabelle had instantly acquired respectability and sympathy — a fact that caused her embarrassment at the deception, but satisfaction that Madeleine would be accepted in the same way as the daughter of any other married woman. Dorothy's friends and acquaintances had readily adopted the young French girl and her mother, and Madeleine was often invited to her school friends' homes and in turn, asked them to play in the apartment above Maison Dubois which they shared with Dorothy.

It wasn't only Madeleine who was popular with Dorothy's social circle. The shop had seen an increase in male customers who would enter, looking about in embarrassment and then enquire about corsages, handbags or some other trinket. It had been Dorothy who worked out why Maison Dubois had suddenly become so popular with male clientèle. Those selecting something for a wife were happy to be served by either Dorothy or Isabelle. However, several gentlemen who regularly came in searching for gifts for sisters, mothers or cousins — never a fiancée or wife — always requested Isabelle's help.

'Hogwash!' Dorothy would say after one of the gentlemen left with a small gift-wrapped item for his mother or sister. 'It's you he's after, my girl! He couldn't take his eyes off you! You could have sold him a coal sack and he'd have been happy!'

Isabelle was flattered, and when one of them finally summoned courage to ask her out on a stroll in the park to the bandstand to listen to the music, she was persuaded to go by her aunt.

But the outing with Hugh Mansfield had been a disaster . . .

'He spent the entire afternoon talking about himself and then . . . ' Isabelle paused, 'He suggested a trip to the coast next weekend.'

'Well? What's wrong with a day at the seaside?'

'No, Dorothy, not a day . . . a night. And when I refused and pointed out that I barely knew him, he said he thought that as I was French, I'd be happy to accept his invitation.'

'The scoundrel! If he dares set foot in Maison Dubois again, I'll give him a piece of my mind!'

'Don't worry, Dorothy, after the telling-off I gave him, he's unlikely ever to come back. I'm afraid I thoroughly insulted one of your clients.'

'Fiddlesticks! Customers like that we can do without! Anyway, takings have increased again this month and we can hardly keep up with orders, so we can do without Mr Hugh Mansfield's custom.'

★ ★ ★

Isabelle accepted several other invitations during the following months. She was escorted to afternoon tea, dinner in the best restaurant in Guildford, and the opera in London, but by the end of the afternoon or evening, she knew she would not be seeing that particular man again.

'Are you sure you're not being a bit too . . . well, fastidious?' Dorothy asked after the latest trip to an art exhibition. 'He seemed like a lovely young man . . . intelligent, funny and rather handsome.'

'I know, Aunt, and you're probably right, but I'm looking for something special . . . a spark or something. Maman and Papa had it. And the way you talk about Uncle Henri, you obviously had it. Do you think I'm being unrealistic?'

'Well, Henri was the first and only man I ever loved, so I'm not really experienced in affairs of the heart. But I don't believe everyone sees stars and rainbows when they first meet someone. It may take time to develop a relationship . . . '

'I suppose so, but there's Madeleine to consider. I've been honest about having a daughter but no one has asked about her, as if they don't want to know. I think it best if I turn down invitations in the future. I couldn't consider a man who could not be a father to my girl.'

'Don't give up completely. They all seem very keen — even Hugh Mansfield wasn't put off by your rejection and scolding. I've seen him sitting at a table in the café opposite watching the shop.'

'It's probably just a coincidence . . . '

★   ★   ★

That night Isabelle was unable to sleep in the oppressive summer heat. Next to her in the double bed, Madeleine tossed and turned, waking when the thunder that had threatened all day began to rumble. Isabelle tried to persuade Madeleine to sleep in her own bed next door but in the end had given way. At times like this, she was glad to be there to calm Madeleine's fears.

If she were to find a man, this closeness with her daughter would have to stop. Perhaps that was reason enough to resign herself to a life alone. Would Madeleine suffer if she didn't have a father? So many died during the war so it wasn't unusual to find fatherless families. Madeleine had her as well as Aunt Dorothy, so she was loved and surely that was the most important thing?

Isabelle thought over the conversation she'd had with her aunt earlier. It was true she was being unrealistic; it was likely the sort of man she wanted simply didn't exist. Madeleine had to come first but how many men wanted another man's child? Several of her suitors had seemed quite childlike and needy themselves. They'd all served in France during the war and their experiences had affected them deeply, not surprising. Having been so close to the Front and having seen the endless stream of wounded, Isabelle had an idea of what they must have gone through and was sympathetic, but they seemed to want something she was unable to provide.

The storm passed and Madeleine was once again asleep, although from time to time thunder grumbled in the distance. Isabelle felt as though she was back in Montplessis during the four years of war when she could hear the explosions on the Front carried on the breeze.

For the first time in months she thought about Lieutenant Tom Marshall and wondered how he'd fared after the war. Lately, Madeleine had started asking questions about her father — what had he been like, was he handsome, why were there no photographs of him in Aunt Dorothy's apartment?

Isabelle had told her she had mislaid the photographs during their move to England, but she had two hidden away. Lying didn't come easily to Isabelle but it was necessary because Madeleine was not yet old enough to understand. One day, she would explain everything and show her the photographs of Tom.

How would Madeleine take the news that she was the illegitimate child of an English officer and not the daughter of a French hero? Well, Isabelle would worry about that when the time came, but for now, she wondered how Tom would react if he ever knew about Madeleine.

Perhaps Sergeant Newman had been wrong and Tom hadn't been married. Perhaps he would like to know he had a daughter — and who could fail to fall in love with such a beautiful little girl? If by some chance he was happy to learn about Madeleine, then perhaps father and daughter could get to know each other. Perhaps, perhaps . . .

She'd wondered many times in the past when she'd studied the photographs, but always returned them to the hiding place at the back of the drawer under the letters from Hélène. She had Tom's address — although it had occurred to her that he might no longer live there — but she couldn't simply knock on his door and introduce Madeleine. That wouldn't be fair, especially if he was married.

So how could she contact him? Suddenly, she realised the photographs would be the key.

She would go to the address in Wimbledon and if Tom answered the door, she would ask if they could meet away from the house and then . . . well, she'd simply tell him and see what happened.

However, if a wife opened the door, she would pretend that the photographer in Beauvais had asked her to deliver the photographs which had been forgotten in his studio and only recently been discovered. She would apologise that her 'photographer friend' had failed to post them but would explain that conditions had been difficult during the war. Then, she would walk away as if her only purpose in calling had been to deliver the photographs as a favour to her friend.

Isabelle decided to ask Dorothy the following day if she would mind her leaving as soon as the shop shut for half day closing, although she thought it best not to mention that she planned to go to Tom's house. She wasn't sure whether her aunt would encourage her or attempt to dissuade her, but either way, Isabelle had made up her mind and nothing would sway her. After all, there could be a variety of reasons for a day out in London and there was no need for her to announce them all to Aunt Dorothy. It would be an opportunity to spend time with her daughter, to go to A J Farrant, a renowned haberdashers near Leicester Square, to look for inspiration for new hat designs, as well as to enjoy afternoon tea in the Lyons Corner House on the Strand.

Madeleine had fizzed with excitement when she'd heard of the proposed trip and Isabelle regretted not keeping it a secret until the day.

'Maman, when we go to the haberdashers, can I buy something for the hat I'm making?'

The following day, Dorothy suggested they leave mid-morning rather than wait until she closed the shop at lunchtime.

Madeleine threw her arms round her great-aunt's neck. 'Thank you, Aunt Dottery!'

'Just have a wonderful time and . . . ' she slipped the little girl a sixpence, 'See what you can buy in Farrant's with that.'

Madeleine kissed her and put the coin in her purse with the pocket money she'd been saving.

The train journey from Guildford was uneventful although everything was a source of wonder to Madeleine who knelt on the seat to get a better view of the countryside and looked at their fellow passenger with enormous, excited eyes.

'Don't stare, Chérie,' Isabelle whispered and tried to distract her daughter from gazing in fascination at a pot-bellied man who sat opposite. Madeleine had obviously never seen anything like his black moustache that was waxed to sharp points on either side of his cheeks. Luckily, the motion of the carriage rocked him to sleep and he didn't notice Madeleine's absorption with his facial hair.

'Is this Waterloo Station, Maman?'

'No, Chérie, we're going to get off before we reach London. I have an errand to run first.' Isabelle took Madeleine's hand and helped her down from the carriage onto the station platform.

'But we will be going to London, won't we, Maman? You haven't changed your mind?'

'No, Chérie.' Isabelle smoothed the fringe off her daughter's forehead out of her eyes. 'We're definitely going to London.'

Isabelle didn't need to check the envelope containing the photographs for Tom's address. She had looked at it so many times during the last six years she knew it by heart.

'Please can you tell me if Queens Road is far?' she asked the guard once he'd waved his flag and blown his whistle to send the steam train on its way.

'Out the station and turn left, ma'am. You can't miss it.'

'Where are we going?' Madeleine asked. She skipped alongside her mother as they walked along the tree-lined road of semi-detached villas.

'I have something to deliver, Chérie.'

'You look sad, Maman. Are you sad?'

'No, Madeleine, I'm fine. Now, I

need you to help me count the numbers of the houses. See, this is number sixty-two and the next one will be sixty-four. We have to keep walking until we come to number ninety-two. Can you help me count?'

'Oh yes, Maman! I'll find it for you.'

Isabelle pretended to blow her nose on a handkerchief and when Madeleine turned to look for the house numbers, she dabbed her eyes. Perhaps this hadn't been a good idea . . .

'Here it is! Shall I ring the doorbell?'

'No! Wait!'

Madeleine froze, shocked at the sharpness of her mother's tone.

'I'm sorry, Chérie, I need to prepare what I have to deliver, that's all. I didn't mean to shout. Come here and wait with me . . . '

The little girl let the gate go and walked back to her mother, tears glinting in her eyes.

'I'm sorry, Maman, I only wanted to help . . . '

'I know, it is I who am sorry. Just let

me get this envelope out of my bag and we'll ring the doorbell together, yes?' Isabelle crouched down and put her arm round Madeleine. She took one of the photographs out of the envelope and slipped it in her bag. 'Right, I'm ready now.' She took Madeleine's hand and after breathing deeply, she opened the gate and walked up the path to the front door of number ninety-two.

★　★　★

Isabelle gasped when she saw the girl who opened the door. She had the same heart-shaped face crowned by chestnut curls as her own daughter — although she appeared to be four or five years older than Madeleine.

'Hello, can I help you?' she asked politely.

'Err, yes, thank you . . . I'm . . . I'm looking for a Mr Tom Marshall. Is this the right house?'

'Yes, that's my pa.'

'Who is it, Joey?' a woman's voice

came from the house.

'Someone looking for Pa.'

A woman appeared behind the girl drying her hands on her apron.

'Yes? Can I help you? I'm Mrs Marshall.'

'Err, yes, I . . . err . . . I believe your husband had this photograph taken when he was serving in France.' She held out the envelope, 'But unfortunately, it was mislaid. My friend found it in his photography studio the other day and since I was coming to London, he asked me to deliver it with his apologies.'

Mrs Marshall looked at the envelope doubtfully.

'I see. And what else are you selling?'

'Nothing. I'm not selling anything. Your husband paid for this photograph when he was in France.'

'I see.' She held out her hand and Isabelle gave her the envelope. When she saw the photograph, she clutched her chest and groaned.

'Are you all right?' Isabelle asked.

'Yes, it's just such a shock to see Tom so young and so . . . well, so alive.'

'Oh no! I'm so sorry, I didn't realise! I'm so sorry for your loss, Mrs Marshall . . . I didn't mean to upset you . . . '

'Oh, no, he's not dead. I'm sorry, I didn't explain myself well at all. No, he survived the war. It's just that when he came home, it was like he'd left part of himself in France.'

Isabelle looked at her in horror.

'Part of himself?' she whispered.

'Yes, our doctor says it's shell shock. He said we're to give Tom time to get over it but I'm beginning to think . . . I'm sorry, what must you think of me, telling you all my troubles?'

'Please don't apologise Mrs Marshall. I lived near the Front, and I saw soldiers like your husband on their way to the trenches and then again after they'd been fighting. I know exactly what you mean.'

'Thank you. I know lots of men are finding it hard to get over their experiences.'

Mrs Marshall showed her daughter the photograph. 'See, Joey, this is Pa when he was fighting in the war. You were just two when he went away. Isn't he handsome in his uniform?'

The girl nodded and looked up at Isabelle.

'Did you know Pa in France?'

Isabelle swallowed. 'There were thousands of British soldiers who passed through my town . . . '

'It must have been very hard for you all,' Mrs Marshall said.

Isabelle nodded. Her throat was constricted and she was finding it hard to speak.

'Where are my manners? Perhaps you and your daughter would like to come in for a cuppa? Go and put the kettle on, Joey.'

'Oh, no, thank you. My daughter and I have a lot to do today, but thank you.'

Tom's wife and daughter seemed like nice people and if Tom was as badly damaged mentally as his wife said, then he probably wouldn't remember her at all. It sounded as though he wasn't coping with his life, so he certainly wouldn't welcome any complications.

She took Madeleine's hand and led her back down the path.

*　　*　　*

There was a thirty-minute wait for the next train to Waterloo Station and Isabelle was grateful that Madeleine asked for her sketchbook and pencils so that she could draw while they sat on the bench on the platform. There was a great deal for Isabelle to mentally process.

The pain in Tom's wife's eyes had shocked Isabelle and she knew she would never risk the woman finding out what had happened that night in the château — or that her husband had another daughter. The Marshall family were obviously dealing with many issues and they had suffered enough. She was relieved that Tom had not come to the door. If he couldn't cope with life at home with his family, then he certainly wouldn't want the complication of another child.

At least now she knew he could never be part of their lives and that Madeleine would remain her secret. A great weight slipped from her shoulders and for the first time she felt content. She had a good home, work she loved, a kind aunt and a beautiful daughter — what more could she ask?

By the time the train pulled into Waterloo station she felt as if she'd been born anew. Today she was going to enjoy her daughter's company and everything London offered them. And tomorrow? Well, tomorrow, she'd wake knowing that she no longer had to search for that indefinable something that had been missing from her life. Because nothing was missing from her life. She had everything she needed.

Isabelle ruffled Madeleine's curls.

'Only five minutes 'til the train comes, Chérie. Why don't you show me what you've drawn?'

The little girl's cheeks reddened.

'I haven't drawn a lot, Maman.'

'Never mind, Chérie, there'll be plenty to draw when we get to London. I bet your fingers won't be able to move fast enough to get all your ideas down on paper!'

The train was nearly full when it pulled into the station, but Isabelle found one seat. She pulled her daughter on to her lap.

'Don't wriggle, Chérie, or you'll kick someone.'

Madeleine sat quietly. The earlier excitement at travelling to London appeared to have dissipated, although by the time they'd found their way to the station exit, she regained her high spirits.

They stopped to admire the Victory Arch, a memorial to the railway employees killed during the Great War, which had been opened by the Queen in 1922. It was several years since Isabelle had visited London and even she was surprised at how crowded the streets were with horse-drawn and motor vehicles. And so many people! Isabelle took Madeleine's hand and held her tightly as she moved into the flow of pedestrians walking towards Westminster Bridge.

'Everything is so big, Maman!' Madeleine's eyes were wide with wonder.

'I know, Chérie. Keep hold of my hand. I'll never find you if we get separated. Look — there's Big Ben!'

The crowds had thinned slightly by the time they arrived at Leicester Square and found A J Farrant in a cobbled backstreet. The tiny shop front belied the large area inside filled with trimmings that drew costumiers from many of the nearby theatres.

Isabelle spent some time selecting ribbons, beads and lace for Maison Dubois. Madeleine clutched the sixpence Aunt Dorothy had given her and the few pence she'd saved, and carefully selected a box of sequins, ribbons, and some exotic feathers. She gazed long-ingly at some Russian veiling net but it cost more than twice the money she had in her fist.

'I'll buy you a little gift, Chérie.'

'Oh, Maman!' Madeleine's eyes lit up as the shop assistant winked at her and placed some of the netting with their other purchases.

'Is that gentleman looking for you?' the shop assistant asked as she held out her hand for the money that Isabelle was counting. She nodded at the shop door where a man was peering through the window into the dim shop. Isabelle swung round to look and just as she caught sight of the man, who was shielding his eyes to help him see into the interior, he appeared to jump and immediately moved away. For a second, Isabelle thought he looked like Hugh Mansfield — but that would have been too much of a coincidence.

Isabelle took her daughter's hand as they left the backstreet and stepped out into busy Leicester Square. There was no sign of the man.

'Where are we going now, Maman?'

'We'll eat our sandwiches here under the trees and then we'll walk to Trafalgar Square. If we save some crumbs, we can feed the pigeons. Then we'll go to the Strand and have afternoon tea. If we don't eat too many cakes, we'll have time to stroll along the Thames on our way home.'

⋆　⋆　⋆

Madeleine's eyelids drooped as she fought to keep them open but the rhythmic motion of the railway carriage soon rocked her to sleep with her head leaning against her mother.

Isabelle, too, was tired after such a full day. What had started out as fraught and difficult had ended up one of the happiest days she had known. Gone was the feeling that something was missing from her life. She had everything she needed.

But there's always a price to pay for

happiness, whispered a small voice at the back of her mind . . .

5

It was still warm when they arrived at the railway station and began to walk to Maison Dubois.

'I can't wait to show Aunt Dottery my drawings. And all the lovely things I bought in Farrant's. You don't think she'll be too tired, do you?'

'No, Chérie, we'll be home by nine. I bet she can't wait to hear all about our trip and see what we bought. She'll probably be watching for us.'

But there was no one waiting at the window of the apartment above Maison Dubois.

'She'll be in the kitchen putting the kettle on.'

But when Isabelle unlocked the door, there was no clinking of cups, no whir of the treadle sewing machine, nor music from Aunt Dorothy's wind-up gramophone.

Fear gripped Isabelle's heart with icy fingers. The house was never silent.

When she reached the sitting room, Aunt Dorothy was sitting in her armchair, head leaning on the wing of her chair, hands resting on the jacket she had been embroidering. Isabelle had seen her in the same position countless times before — but this was different. Dorothy's face was still and waxy, and Isabelle knew when she touched her skin that it would be cold.

★   ★   ★

'Leave Guildford? Leave Maison Dubois? Maman! What would we do in France? Would you buy a shop?' Madeleine asked, a little afraid.

Isabelle shook her head sadly. 'We can't afford to do anything like that.'

'But Aunt Dottery said Maison Dubois was doing really well,' Madeleine said.

'It was . . . it is. But it doesn't belong to us.'

80

Even if she could afford a shop, there would be no point buying anything in Montplessis where she knew from Hélène's letters that her name was still tainted with scandal. Perhaps she could rent somewhere small in Paris where she knew no one. But that was the problem — she didn't know anyone — how could she start afresh with no customers?

Madeleine looked at her, eyes wide with dread.

'Then what shall we do, Maman?'

She'd never seen her mother so full of doubt.

'You're not to worry, Chérie.' She kissed the top of Madeleine's head. 'I'll sort this out.'

Suddenly, seeing the world through her daughter's eyes, she realised how little Madeleine knew about the country of her birth. Or indeed the circumstances of her birth.

Not yet. She's too young, she told herself.

'Perhaps Aunt Dottery's brother will

let us stay on here, Maman . . . '

Isabelle knew he wouldn't. Dorothy and Charles had disliked each other — he disapproved of his sister marrying a Frenchman — and despite knowing that Isabelle and Madeleine had been living with Dorothy for several years, he failed to inform them of the date of the funeral.

It was only by chance that Father Cuthbert mentioned it to Isabelle when he dropped by to see how she was coping with the loss of her aunt. He was appalled when he realised that Charles had deliberately tried to exclude them.

'Perhaps it's best we don't go, Father. I wouldn't want to upset him.'

'Nonsense, my child! You and Madeleine have as much right to mourn her passing and to say goodbye as he does. In fact, probably more right to mourn your aunt than him. You were there for her. That man was not. Please come. I will deal with any unpleasantness.'

But there had been no unpleasant-ness. During the service, Charles had simply ignored them both. However, as they had walked away from the graveside, hand in hand, he'd inter-cepted them.

'I shall expect you out of the shop by the end of the week. And don't even think about taking anything that belonged to my sister. Leave the key at Dorothy's solicitor.'

'How could Aunt Dottery have such a horrid man for a brother?' Madeleine whispered.

With robes billowing, Father Cuth-bert rushed to them like a concerned mother hen.

'Sufficient unto the day, my children,' he said, watching Charles march out of the graveyard.

'What did he mean, Maman?' Madeleine whispered after Father Cuthbert had left.

'I've no idea, Chérie, but he said he'd pray for us, so I think he was being kind.'

Isabelle offered up a silent prayer of her own. She and Madeleine needed a miracle now . . .

★   ★   ★

The rest of the week was spent packing their belongings. Before Isabelle had a chance to take the key to Dorothy's solicitor, Mr Biddle, he telephoned to ask her to attend a meeting the following day at his office. She assumed that Charles had complained despite giving her until the end of the week to hand over the key, but she was soon to discover that Charles had much more to be aggrieved about than the lack of a key. It seemed Dorothy had concealed her heart problem from everyone but, being aware she might suffer a heart attack at any time, she'd drawn up a will — and had left everything to Isabelle.

'Don't think you're going to get away with this! I'll not let you walk away with my inheritance. I'll see you in court!'

Charles snarled as he walked out of the office and slammed the door.

'Don't worry, my dear,' said Mr Biddle. 'He hasn't a leg to stand on. Mrs Dubois' will is watertight. She made sure of that. And now it all belongs to you.'

* * *

Although Madeleine helped out in Maison Dubois before and after school, Isabelle quickly found that she couldn't cope with all the orders on her own and placed a notice in the window for a seamstress and shop assistant.

Several women applied but if their sewing samples were good their personalities didn't seem suited to shop work, and if they had an aptitude for sales their sewing was poor. Isabelle was beginning to wonder if her expectations were too high. She would give it another week and then decide which was most important — a skilled seamstress or a gifted sales lady, because it seemed no one possessed both sets of skills.

One particularly busy morning, Isabelle was trying to serve two very important customers when a third woman entered the shop. Her green coat and cloche hat were obviously expensive, although Isabelle noted with the eyes of a professional that they were beginning to show signs of wear. A kiss curl of ginger hair protruded from each side of the hat and lay against her cheeks, giving her a doll-like appearance.

'I'm not sure if I prefer the red or the black,' one of the customers said to Isabelle, holding a pair of gloves in each hand and looking from one to the other. 'Perhaps I should take both . . . or, no — what about the beige ones?'

'Are you going to be long, Madame Maréchal? I don't think this hat is right. I need your advice.'

'If you don't mind, ma'am,' the woman in the green coat said to the lady holding the hat, 'I think it would look better if your hair was swept up on the other side to balance it out.'

'Really? You mean like this?'

'Well, if you'd just allow me . . . '

Scooping up the lady's hair, she took some pins from her pocket and deftly inserted them to hold it in place. Then she settled the hat at just the right angle.

'Why, that's perfect! How did you know?' the lady said peering at herself in the mirror.

'I used to dress the hair of the models at Jean-Luc Maurier's in Paris . . . for a while.'

'*The* Jean-Luc Maurier? The fashion designer?'

'Yes.'

'How wonderful! Did you meet him?'

'Oh yes, he liked to keep an eye on his girls . . . and his creations.'

'You must have seen wonderful designs!'

'Yes, I even worked on some of them.'

'You did?'

'I worked in the sewing department.'

'You did? How astonishing!'

'Well, not really. Now . . . ' she said taking a tendril of hair and allowing it to fall onto the woman's face, 'If you let a curl hang in front of your ear, like this . . . '

'Superb! It looks perfect.' The woman turned her head to admire it in the mirror from all angles.

The other customer — now with three pairs of gloves in front of her — turned as if to ask for help from the woman in the green coat who nodded her approval.

'I'll take all three,' she said handing them to Isabelle proudly as if her taste had been approved by a fashion expert.

'I can't thank you enough,' Isabelle said when the customers had left the shop. 'Now, how can I help you? I'd be very happy if you'd accept a small token of my gratitude.'

'Well, actually, I didn't come in to buy. I came in to enquire about the job.'

'It's yours!' said Isabelle. 'Anyone who worked for Jean-Luc Maurier and who could persuade Mrs Brewster to make up her mind without saying a word is a welcome addition to Maison Dubois!'

*   *   *

Flora Baines proved to be the perfect employee. She was punctual, courteous and dedicated. Even better, she and Madeleine adored each other. The only misgiving Isabelle had was that Flora was very private and rarely spoke about her past. But then Isabelle seldom spoke about her life before she'd arrived in England.

Flora told her she had moved from a small village in the Highlands to stay with her cousin in Guildford so she could find work in London, but after seeing Maison Dubois's shop window and the advertised job, she'd changed her mind about working in the capital. Other than that she'd had several jobs in Edinburgh before working in Paris for Jean-Luc Maurier, Isabelle knew little else.

'Do you think Flora will leave soon, Maman?' Madeleine asked several months after their assistant had first arrived.

'I hope not, Chérie! What on earth makes you ask that? Has she said anything about leaving?'

'Oh no, it's just that she said she loved working for Jean-Luc Maurier but she only stayed with him a while. She didn't stay long in that big house in Edinburgh either. Perhaps she doesn't like staying in one place for long. I'd be very sad if she left.'

'Me too. I've come to rely on her a lot.'

One morning when Isabelle noticed Flora looking through the classified adverts in the newspaper, she feared the worst. 'Please tell me you're not looking for another job, Flora.'

'Job? Oh no, I'm looking for a room. My cousin has been hinting for some time that her house is too small for all of us. She's expecting her fifth baby, so I really think it's time I found somewhere of my own. But I can't afford any of these,' she said pointing at the adverts.

'You're very welcome to move in with Madeleine and me if you like. We've plenty of room.'

* * *

Word soon got around that Isabelle's new employee had worked for Jean-Luc Maurier, and the connection with the great designer enhanced the reputation of Maison Dubois and increased its clientèle.

Several of the men who'd previously asked Isabelle out on social engagements made it clear they were still interested in her, including Hugh Mansfield, who apologised for his ill-judged invitation to the seaside and his comments about her being French. But despite Flora's encouragement,

Isabelle refused all social invitations, even though Flora also rejected any offers to take her out for the evening.

Several times Isabelle had pursued the matter but Flora shrugged off the comments.

'You always turn men down, Izzy,' she said.

'Yes, but I have to consider Madeleine.'

'And would you accept their offers if Madeleine wasn't a factor?'

'Probably not. I learned some time ago that love has no fairytale endings. But you could go out and have fun. Why don't you?'

'So far, no one's been my cup of tea.'

Isabelle knew she would get no further explanation.

★　★　★

It wasn't until December, 1930, that Isabelle discovered the reason for Flora's lack of interest in the men who'd asked her to go out . . .

Madeleine helped her mother and Flora with sewing dresses and decorating hats in her free time. She would be fourteen years old the following year and couldn't wait to leave school to work in Maison Dubois full time, although Isabelle had encouraged her to find an office job where she could work with girls her own age.

The weeks leading up to Christmas had been particularly busy as they had been asked to make fancy-dress costumes as well as the usual cocktail dresses and smart outfits. Isabelle had engaged several seamstresses to help with the extra orders. Nevertheless, they had been struggling to serve all the customers, and on the Saturday before Christmas, Flora suggested they have sherry and mince pies in the shop to keep everyone happy while they waited. She'd baked several batches of pies which Isabelle arranged on platters and placed them beside the sherry bottles and glasses.

By the end of the day, they'd sold out

of gloves, scarves and purses, and completed all the orders. It had been a spectacular success for the business although they were all too tired and to cook dinner. Isabelle made sandwiches and they'd finished off the mince pies and sherry around the fire in the apartment.

'I can't wait to work here full time, Maman.'

Isabelle sighed. 'I wish you'd think again.'

'But I love working here! Please don't try to put me off. It's the only thing keeping me going!'

'Yes, I know you want to work here, Chérie. It's just that I'm not sure it's good to spend all your time with two middle-aged women.' Isabelle glanced in Flora's direction, hiding her smile.

'Middle-aged? You know how to make a woman feel old, Izzy!'

'Well, I don't think I'd like to work with people my age. I much prefer being here than at school,' said Madeleine.

'But don't you think it would be lovely to have some nice new girl-friends, Chérie? And in a few years, you might meet a young man . . . '

'I don't think I'd like to meet a young man.'

'But you might in a few years. You don't want to stay single all your life.'

'You and Flora are. Why do I need a man?'

Flora and Isabelle exchanged worried glances.

'Maddie darling, it's different for us. Your mother's been married and I . . . ' She paused as if wondering whether to continue. 'I was almost married. My fiancé, Peter . . . ' She swallowed and it took her a few seconds before she could continue. 'Peter died in the war. That's how I came to work in Paris for a while. I went to France to look for him. I found him in a hospital but he was so badly wounded . . . he died in my arms.'

'Flora, I'm so sorry! How terrible for you!'

'Peter was the love of my life. If I can't have him, I don't want anyone. But you, Maddie, you're young and one day I hope you'll fall in love.'

'Oh Flora, I had no idea,' said Isabelle.

'It's not something I like to talk about and it didn't seem fair to remind you of losing your husband. But I wouldn't want Maddie to think that just because we aren't married that she shouldn't consider it. I hope she'll find someone and be as happy as I was with Pete. And as happy as you were with your husband.'

The lump in Isabelle's throat prevented her from answering. She hated the deceit but there was no way she could tell Flora her secret — not now she knew about Flora's fiancé. But one thing was certain, it was time to tell Madeleine. She was thirteen years old and she deserved to know about her father.

'Well, I think I've had enough sherry,' Flora said, standing up. 'I'm off to bed.

I'm exhausted. Thank goodness it's Sunday tomorrow.'

Isabelle placed a restraining hand on Madeleine's arm when she rose to go to her bedroom. Once Flora's footsteps could be heard on the stairs, she said, 'Wait, Chérie. I think it's time I told you about your father . . . '

★　★　★

Christmas had not been the joyful occasion that Isabelle and Madeleine usually shared. Flora received a letter telling her that her mother had been taken ill a few days before Christmas and she'd gone back to Scotland to help her family.

After learning about her father, Madeleine had retreated into herself. She'd been grateful that her mother had finally told her the truth but shocked that so much had been kept from her. Isabelle had apologised repeatedly and they had both cried, but it felt as though their closeness had been built on lies and Madeleine grieved — for the French father who'd never been, for the relationship she'd once had with her mother, and for the English father who apparently had a family of his own and didn't want her. She wasn't sure if she'd rather not have known about her real father and for some time, she refused to look at the photograph that Isabelle gave her.

By the time Flora returned to Guildford, Madeleine had almost made up her mind to try to find a job in an office so that at least she'd be away from the shop most of the day. Relations between her and her mother had been strained and she knew it would only be a matter of time before Flora picked up on the tension. Of all the people in the world, Madeleine would have trusted Flora with the news about her father but something held her back. To discuss it would make it real, and Madeleine preferred the story that she'd always believed. Anyway, Flora had been very distracted when she returned. Her mother had died and she was obviously struggling to deal with her loss.

'I didn't even get on with my mother,' she said with tears coursing down her cheeks. 'I couldn't do anything right in her eyes. But now she's gone . . . now she's gone . . . I wish I'd tried harder.'

'I'm sure she was proud of you in her way,' said Isabelle, putting her arm round Flora's shoulders.

'You only get one mother . . . I wish I'd . . . ' Flora couldn't finish for the tears.

Madeleine had never seen such raw grief and for a second she felt ashamed of the resentment she'd held towards her own mother. Suppose something happened to Isabelle? Wouldn't she regret having been so cold towards her? Would it have made it any easier if Madeleine had known about her father years ago? Probably not. She wouldn't have understood and might have told someone. Once a secret like that was out, it could never be reclaimed. And the pretence had been for her benefit. How might her school days have been different if she'd been known as the French woman's bastard? No, her mother had acted in her best interests — she'd even left her home and her own mother for Madeleine's sake.

Isabelle had an arm round the sobbing Flora as Madeleine slipped her hand into her mother's. 'You only get one mother,' she whispered.

Tears of relief ran down Isabelle's cheeks and she gripped her daughter's hand tightly.

By the time Madeleine left school and started work full time at Maison Dubois, it was as though she'd never discovered the truth about her father.

Why spare a thought for a man who had no interest in her or in her mother? She would forget him. Yet it seemed the more she tried to ignore him, the more she wondered what he was like. Isabelle had given her the photograph taken in the studio at Beauvais but she had refused to look at it and her mother had taken it back and hidden it in a drawer, beneath the letters that Mémé sent from Montplessis.

Did she resemble her father? It surely wouldn't hurt to get the photograph and look — after all, Maman had offered it to her before. At the first opportunity, Madeleine took the envelope from the drawer, slipped it in her pocket and took it to her room. She wasn't sure why she felt so guilty — her mother had had given her ample opportunity to look at the photo — but she wanted to keep her thoughts private.

When she was sure her mother and Flora were downstairs in the shop, she locked the door and slid the photograph out of the envelope.

Lieutenant Tom Marshall.

She had wondered if she'd feel anything — love, anger, disappointment — but instead, the photograph triggered a memory . . .

She must have been five or six and

she remembered skipping at her mother's side along an unfamiliar, tree-lined street, counting house numbers. Her mother had been disturbed — she'd known that, although she didn't know why — and then they'd knocked at the door of one of the houses. Maman had spoken to the woman although Madeleine couldn't remember the conversation because she was studying the girl who had opened the door and was standing next to the woman.

For a second, Madeleine had had the strange feeling that she was looking into a mirror but the more she looked, the less like her the girl seemed. Yes, they had similarly coloured curly hair but no one would say they looked like each other — and yet, there was a resemblance.

The girl's attention had turned to Madeleine and she knew she'd been caught staring. With flaming cheeks, she'd moved closer to her mother and half hidden behind her skirt feeling very naïve and childish. This confident older girl wouldn't have skipped along the road calling out house numbers. She would have walked sensibly and not been over-eager to knock at the door, earning a sharp word from her mother.

Madeleine concentrated on remembering every detail of that day. The girl would probably have been almost as old as Madeleine was now. Her mother had called her Joey; Madeleine remembered that because it was also the name of the next-door neighbour's cat. She also remembered the house was number ninety-two although she wasn't sure of the name of the road in Wimbledon . . . but she remembered how to get there from the station.

Why had the photograph triggered such a memory? It finally came to her when her mind was drifting from wakefulness that night and she sat up in bed, all thoughts of sleep banished.

Maman had given the woman a photograph, like the one that she'd put back under Mémé's letters. The woman had drawn Joey's attention to the photograph, remarking how handsome her father was.

Joey's father. Her father.

A tingle went through her. She had been only yards from her real father and had been staring at her half-sister! How had she not known? Well, of course she couldn't have known! She'd been much too young to suspect anything like that.

Now she longed to see her half-sister and perhaps even her father, although she knew he wasn't aware of her existence — and it was probably best it remained that way. If Maman hadn't told him, there must have been a good reason. Perhaps she should ask her?

Madeleine knew she wouldn't. When Isabelle had told her about her father, she'd glossed over exactly what had happened when she was conceived, but she had expressed her deep shame and had apologised profusely. It was shocking to see her mother so upset, so it was best that she wasn't reminded of the whole thing.

So how could Madeleine find out more?

She'd do what her mother had done. She'd go to her father's house and on some pretext and talk to her half-sister. Just talk. Nothing more.

★ ★ ★

The opportunity came several weeks later when Flora remarked that she needed some peacock-blue lace and matching ribbon and she was annoyed that their usual suppliers in Guildford had nothing close to the colour she wanted. Madeleine's heart beat faster as she suggested someone should go to Farrant's in London, knowing that both Isabelle and Flora were busy with orders.

'Yes,' said Flora, 'Farrant's is bound to have some but I can't spare the time to go.'

'I'll go,' Madeleine said casually.

'On your own, Chérie?'

'Yes, of course, Maman. Flora only

has two days to finish that dress and she needs the lace.'

'Well, I suppose it would be very helpful. Do you think you'll be able to get there on your own?'

'Of course! I've been lots of times with you. I won't get lost.'

Madeleine set off early the following day, running to the station to make sure she caught a very early train. She wanted plenty of time in Wimbledon, and of course she had to make sure she got to Leicester Square to buy the lace and ribbon. Maman had given her a list of things to get and normally she would have been delighted to browse in Farrant's — but today she was trying to recall the route she had taken with Maman the last time they'd been to Wimbledon.

Suppose she couldn't find the house? Or what if the Marshalls didn't live there any more?

As she left the station, it was just as she remembered it. The canopies of the trees that lined the street cast deep shadow on the pavement as Madeleine walked briskly along, looking for number ninety-two. The house seemed slightly more tired than she remembered, and the paint on the door was scratched and worn around the keyhole and door knob.

She rang the doorbell and waited; her heart pounding. She would pretend she was looking for a friend and that she had been given their address. She would do her best to keep them talking but if necessary, she was prepared to act as if she felt faint and hope she was invited into the house for a glass of water.

Nothing would persuade her to reveal who she was but it would be wonderful to be with her father and sister even if only for a few minutes.

The door opened, bringing her back to reality.

'Yes?' a woman with a cigarette dangling from her lips answered the door.

'Oh, um, I was looking for the

Marshall family.'

'They don't live 'ere anymore.' The woman started to close the door.

'No, wait, please! Do you know where they went?' Madeleine pleaded.

'Why should I tell you?'

'They're relatives. Please, I must find them!'

'Well, all right.' The woman seemed to soften slightly. 'I think I've got their address somewhere. They moved out last year when Mr Marshall died. I don't think his wife and daughter could afford the rent And I'm not surprised. Bloomin' landlord charges a fortune!'

Madeleine swayed slightly. There was no need for pretence for she really did feel faint.

'You all right, love? D'you want to come in? You've gone really white. You can come in and rest for a bit if you like, love.'

But after the initial shock Madeleine had recovered and was keen to know if the woman had Mrs Marshall's new address. If it wasn't far, she might be able to find it. But the address was in Stepney in the east end of London and Madeleine knew she wouldn't have time to get to Leicester Square as well as look for the Marshall's house.

She didn't remember the walk back to the station, nor boarding the train for Waterloo. How cruel to have missed seeing her father by a few months. And now she might even have lost the opportunity to meet her sister.

* * *

'Are you all right, Chérie? You seem very down,' Isabelle remarked to Madeleine later that evening. 'Are you tired?'

'No Maman, I'm fine, really.' Madeleine arranged a smile on her face and tried to look happy. If Isabelle thought the day had been too much for her, she wouldn't let Madeleine go to London on her own again — and at the first opportunity she planned to get to Stepney and search for her sister.

She had to wait a further two weeks before Isabelle needed something from Farrant's. Madeleine tried to conceal her eagerness as she suggested she should go because everyone else was so busy.

'Well, if you don't mind, Chérie, that would be a great help,'

'No, I don't mind at all.'

One of the part-time seamstresses originally came from Whitechapel and without explaining that she intended to travel to the East End, Madeleine managed to find out which omnibus to get. She wasn't sure where to get off, but it couldn't be that hard, could it?

People were helpful and despite her fears at getting lost, she found herself in Aylward Street looking for number ten.

This street was very different from the leafy suburban road where the Marshall family had lived in Wimbledon. The front doors of the grey, terraced houses opened straight on to the pavement and small children, spilled out of the houses while women scrubbed steps and chatted to each other across the street. There was a scruffy, tired air about Aylward Street although it seemed friendly enough.

One house stood out as being smarter than the rest. There was a vase of flowers in the downstairs window and its door was closed as if it was trying to ignore the noisy neighbours. Madeleine checked the scrap of paper on which the address was written, although she knew it off by heart. Number ten, Aylward Street. She took a deep breath and raised the knocker. She suddenly realised that many of the women had fallen silent and were watching her.

'Cor, you're brave!' one young boy said as he ran past bouncing a ball.

Before she could be sure he was talking to her, the door opened.

'Yes.' The woman's voice was cold and the eyes narrowed with suspicion.

'Um, I'm sorry to bother you but I'm looking for Mrs Marshall.'

'Try the cemetery.' She closed the door.

How rude! Madeleine knocked again.

'Please! It's really important I find Mrs Marshall or Miss Marshall.'

'Go away.' The door was slammed and Madeleine heard the bolt being drawn.

So, that was it.

If the woman was to be believed, Mrs Marshall had also died, so Joey could be anywhere. The trail had gone cold.

Madeleine's eyes filled with tears.

'Excuse me, lovey. I couldn't help overhearing you're looking for Rose Marshall.' A stout woman with curlers in her hair covered by a scarf beckoned from the door of the house next door. 'You won't get any information out of Ivy.' She nodded at number ten. 'She couldn't stand Rose and Joanna. Mind you, she can't stand anyone.'

'Do you know anything about them?'

'I spoke to Rose a few times before she died. She weren't here long. Such a shame it were. Joanna was devastated at losing her ma so soon after her pa. So sudden too. One morning she went off to work and by lunch time she were gone. So sad for poor Joanna. You didn't know then, about Rose passing on I mean?'

'No, I've only just found out they're distant relatives and I was trying to find them.'

'Distant relatives eh? Well, why don't you come in for a cuppa and tell me all about it?'

6

Mrs Thomsett from number twelve, Aylward Street had been very helpful. She'd made Madeleine tea and had told her about Ivy, her disagreeable neighbour. Ivy's husband John had invited his sister and niece to live with them when they could no longer afford the rent on their house in Wimbledon, but he was often away on business and hadn't realised that his wife was making his sister's life unpleasant. Rose had confided in Mrs Thomsett that she had plans to buy a house for herself and Joanna in Essex.

'It were all hush-hush,' Mrs Thomsett said, 'Rose wanted to get Joanna away from Ivy's nastiness but before she could sort it all out, she passed away, God rest her soul.'

'Do you know what happened to Joanna?'

'As far as I know, she went to find the house, but she hasn't been back since. Not surprising. I heard the rumpus Ivy made the morning Joanna left. Told her not to come back.'

'I don't suppose you have the address . . .'

'No, sorry. The only thing I know is that it was in Dunton, on the Plotlands there.'

'Where's Dunton?'

'I've never been but it's somewhere out in the wilds of Essex. I know a few people who've got weekend places in Dunton Plotlands. It's quite the thing to do. I asked my Wilf if 'e'd like a place down there but we've got so many little 'uns to look after it'd be 'ard to get away at the weekend. My kids just keep 'aving kids of their own. Every time I look round, there's a new one!'

'Would anyone else know Joanna's address?'

'No, I've already asked. I wondered 'ow she were getting on but she was 'ere for such a short time, no one really knew her. Shame. I'd love to know that she was happy. She didn't deserve such a miserable aunt as Ivy. But she wasn't a country girl. My guess is she sold up, came back to London and got a job here. I could ask a few people if they know anything. Perhaps if you pass this way again, you could call in for a cuppa and I might have some news for you.'

'That's really kind, Mrs Thomsett, I'll try to come back in a few weeks.'

★   ★   ★

Madeleine never went back to Aylward Street.

When she got home from London, Isabelle was packing. She'd received a letter from Madame Picard. Having slipped on the smooth stone stairs in the château one evening, Hélène had lain unconscious at the bottom until Madame Picard found her the following morning and run to get help. Although cold, dehydrated and in a great deal of pain, Hélène had only

116

sprained her wrist and suffered grazing and bruising. But several days later, she'd succumbed to pneumonia.

Isabelle left the running of Maison Dubois in the hands of Madeleine and Flora. It was almost running itself, having a loyal clientèle who kept them busy and financially secure, and so she was able to take a substantial amount of money with her to France, anticipating that the château would be more dilapidated than it had been the last time she and Madeleine had visited, and that it would need some attention.

She had no idea how long it would be before she could either bring Hélène back to England, or if she refused to come, when she would be well enough to be left on her own. The thought that perhaps Hélène might not be well enough for Isabelle to leave her and to return to Guildford was one that she would not allow to worry her. She would deal with whatever situation she found when she got to Montplessis.

By the time Isabelle arrived at the

château, Hélène was feeling much better and many of her bruises had faded to a dull yellow. She was delighted to see Isabelle but irritated with Madame Picard for worrying her daughter and bringing her away from her life in England.

'I'm fine, Chérie! What a shame to have dragged you all the way here. As you can see, I'm on the mend.'

She was definitely looking better but Isabelle was shocked at how frail she seemed and suspected she hadn't been eating properly.

The château was also a cause for concern because during a particularly stormy night a few months before, many of the roof tiles had become dislodged and when it rained heavily, water trickled down the wall of Hélène's bedroom so she had moved into another, much smaller room. Madame Picard asked her brother-in-law Étienne, who was a carpenter, if he would be able to repair the roof and he had arrived the following day to inspect the job and to give her an estimate of the cost. Isabelle had agreed to his price but was dismayed that he would not be able to start for another week.

'It'll be two weeks before we see him again,' Hélène predicted. 'He's good but very slow.'

Isabelle went into the attic and did her best to patch the gaping hole in the roof with canvas in the hope that it would hold back some of the water if it rained. Thankfully, during the next two weeks, the weather was dry and Isabelle began to clean out Hélène's bedroom in the hope that Étienne would arrive and begin proper repairs.

Each morning when Madame Picard arrived at the château, Isabelle asked if she had any news about when Étienne would finally come.

'He will come,' she said, usually with a shrug, as if Isabelle was being unreasonable in expecting him to arrive any time soon.

One morning, Isabelle decided to tackle Hélène's bedroom as it had dried out during the good weather. She intended to clean it thoroughly and to wash the stained curtains to remove the watermarks. Part of the ceiling had collapsed, and she was covered in a fine layer of dust and plaster from sweeping up when she heard the crunch of tyres on the gravel of the drive.

At last, Étienne had come! She was tempted to let him know she was annoyed that he had kept her waiting for so long but as she rushed down the stairs to let him in, she decided to be polite in case he got back in his van and drove off!

The doorbell rang and she opened the door with a fixed smile on her face — which slipped when she realised the man standing on the doorstep wasn't Étienne.

'Have I caught you at a bad time?' he asked in French, although she thought she detected a slight foreign accent.

'No, sorry, I was expecting someone else,' she said realising how disappointed she must look.

'Sorry to bother you,' he said and turning, he walked away.

'Can I help you?' she asked, sorry for being so unwelcoming. 'Are you lost?'

He turned back, 'No, in fact I found the château easily. I wondered whether Madame Rousseau still lived here.'

'Yes, she does. Do you know my mother?'

'Your mother?' He fixed Isabelle with his green eyes. Suddenly recognition lit them up, 'Mademoiselle Rousseau? I remember you.'

'You do?' She searched his face but couldn't place it at all. She would surely have remembered someone so handsome.

7

He swept his dark fringe off his face and smiled at her. 'Don't worry, you won't remember me. I was a Sergeant in the Essex Regiment. I was billeted over there.' He pointed towards the barn. 'And I remember you and your mother helping in the dressing station in town. I was just another Tommy,' he added sadly, shaking his head as if to banish memories. 'I was passing and I thought I'd stop and pay my respects,' he added.

'Please, come in,' Isabelle said, wiping her hands on her apron and raising a cloud of dust, 'Oh, I'm so sorry, I'm trying to clean up my mother's bedroom. The roof's leaking and part of the ceiling's collapsed.' She stopped, realising she was talking too much.

'I'm sorry to have bothered you,' he said 'I can see you're busy. Perhaps you'd convey my respects and thanks to your mother for me.'

'Isabelle, who is it?' Hélène suddenly appeared from the kitchen.

'Sergeant James Hart, Madame,' he said, stepping forward. 'I don't suppose you remember me but I certainly remember you and your daughter. I was billeted in your barn and you also wrote letters home for me when I was wounded.'

Hélène peered at him, then shook her head.

'No, I don't remember, but please come in. Anyone who fought on the Somme deserves our deepest thanks and respect. Come in, come in! I'll make coffee, or tea if you prefer.'

'Thank you — tea would be lovely if you're sure I'm not disturbing you.'

As he entered the hall, thunder rumbled on the horizon and Isabelle groaned.

'Oh no! A storm! That's all we need!'

'Perhaps it won't come this way, Chérie,' said Hélène looking apprehensively at the grey clouds.

'If it does, the canvas won't keep the rain out of your bedroom — and it's only just dried out.'

'Is there anything I can do?' James asked, 'I'm not a carpenter but I'm quite practical.'

'Perhaps you could look at it for us,' said Hélène, 'and I'll put the kettle on for tea.'

Isabelle led the way upstairs and as she entered Hélène's bedroom, she caught sight of herself in the mirror over the fireplace. She'd scraped her hair back off her face into an unflattering bun and wore an old dress and one of Madame Picard's enormous aprons, all covered in grey plaster dust. How dreadful she looked!

With surprise, she realised she cared that this handsome man had seen her at her worst. She thought of Hugh Mansfield and the other men who had taken her out. She had no interest in their opinions — of her, or anything else — but for some reason, this man's opinion mattered.

Not that he was taking any notice of her. He was staring up at what had once been an ornate ceiling but now had an ugly gaping hole which revealed the attic space above and the canvas she had tied up to cover the hole in the roof.

'Can you show me where I can get into the attic?' He took his jacket off and laid it on a chair.

Isabelle led him along the hall to the door leading to the attic. There was a ladder up there but Isabelle had been too short to reach the highest point of the hole and the canvas flapped in the wind. It revealed the sky was becoming darker and it was certain to bring heavy rain.

James climbed to the top of the ladder holding a piece of wood, a hammer, and a pocket full of nails. He managed to trap the canvas behind the wood which he nailed to the rafters, making a much neater job than Isabelle. The sky could no longer be seen but it was obviously raining because fat drops fell on the canvas and rolled down the roof. Amazingly, nothing seemed to be coming into the attic.

'I don't think it'll hold for long,' said James looking up at the makeshift repair, 'I hope your carpenter comes soon.'

It wasn't until they'd got back into the hall that Isabelle saw how dirty James was. His white shirt was covered in debris which had been dislodged while he'd been hammering, and his trousers were smeared with algae which had been thriving in the damp conditions.

Hélène raised her hands in horror when they reappeared in the kitchen.

'Monsieur Hart! Your clothes! I am so sorry! Here, sit down and have your tea. Were you on your way to anywhere important?'

'No, only to find a hotel or a room for a few weeks. Don't worry, I have my suitcase in the car, I can easily get changed.'

'Where are you going? Paris?' Hélène asked.

'No, I hoped to stay in Montplessis or nearby. Can you recommend anywhere?'

Isabelle knew what her mother was going to say before she'd even opened her mouth. Generous Hélène wouldn't send him on his way when she could offer him a bed — but gone were the days when a room in the château was a luxury. Now everything was shabby and dank and Isabelle was certain James wouldn't want to stay.

'Then you must stay here — I insist!'

'Maman!' said Isabelle, 'It's so damp and . . . '

'I certainly wouldn't want to put you to any inconvenience,' James said.

'It's no inconvenience,' Isabelle said quickly, 'It's just that there's been so much storm damage, and the château isn't the place it once was. But you're welcome to stay if you'd like.'

His face lit up, 'That would certainly save me looking for a hotel, thank you. I promise won't get in your way. I'll be out most of the day.'

'Are you working in the area?' Hélène asked.

'No . . . ' he looked down into his teacup, 'I've come back to try to put some memories to rest.'

'Ah,' said Hélène. 'The war . . . '

James nodded. 'I lost so many friends . . . '

Hélène said brightly, 'Chérie, why don't you show Monsieur Hart to one of the guest bedrooms. I'll let Madame Picard know there'll be one more for dinner.'

There were three bedrooms which had been cleaned and were ready to use. Isabelle slept in one and Hélène's was next door. She showed him to the third bedroom which was next to her mother's and returned a few minutes later with fresh linen — but the room was empty. She made the bed, thinking he'd gone down to the car to fetch his suitcase. Looking out of the window, she saw the car wasn't there and assumed he'd parked it at the back of the château.

Once she'd made sure his room was ready, she left and headed straight for her own room to prepare for dinner.

She wore her favourite casual dress and secured her thick, dark hair off her face with two pearl-studded hair combs, allowing it to fall loosely around her shoulders. She didn't want to make it obvious she'd dressed up, but on the other hand, she didn't want James to think she always looked the way she had earlier in the day.

He obviously noted the difference in her appearance when he came down to dinner as his eyes roved over her as if he'd never seen her before, although he'd gallantly complemented both women.

Hélène skilfully steered the conversation at the meal, avoiding any mention of the war, and James seemed to be happy not to refer to his time fighting. He explained that he'd returned home briefly in 1918 to his family and spent

Christmas with them but his father had wanted him to take over the family printing firm. James didn't want his future mapped out for him and had moved to London where he trained to become an architect — something he'd always longed to do. On a holiday in Caen, Normandy, he'd met the director of an architectural company. The two men had become firm friends and when James had been offered a job there, he'd jumped at the chance. For the last fourteen years he'd lived and worked in Caen.

'You never married?' asked Hélène.

'A few near misses,' he said and laughed.

Isabelle looked down at her bare hands. She'd removed the wedding ring she wore in England — there had been no point in France since no one visited the château. She wondered if he was dismissing her as an ageing spinster living with her mother in the French countryside. Strangely, the thought that he might dismiss her hurt.

The same thought may have occurred to Hélène, who said, 'So, you are English and you live in France, and my daughter is French and usually lives in England.'

Isabelle then briefly explained that she had moved to England to stay with her aunt and she now owned a ladies' fashion shop in Guildford.

'I hear it's a great success,' said Hélène. 'As soon as we have made the château weather-tight, we will close it down and then I am going with Isabelle to stay there.'

'You're leaving France?' he asked Isabelle.

'Maman can't stay here on her own and I can't keep away from the shop for much longer. I have a manager and . . . ' She almost said daughter, but she didn't want to have to explain anything to this stranger and she certainly didn't want to lie about being widowed. 'And . . . commitments,' she said finally. 'But I can't leave them indefinitely.'

Isabelle was suddenly reminded of that last meal with Lieutenant Tom Marshall all those years ago, how the conversation had danced around the bloodshed taking place a few miles away along the banks of the River Somme and the absence of Captain Western at the table.

Her thoughts then turned to that brief encounter with Tom which, with such naïvety, she had completely misunderstood. She had vowed never to regret that night — after all, it had led to Madeleine — nevertheless, it had been an event which had coloured her opinions of men ever since. She had prided herself on not needing a man, but there was something about this man that was strangely compelling. His green eyes with their long dark lashes were mesmerising but she detected none of the lascivious looks she'd received from men in the past. He was either unaware of his good looks or simply not interested in her. She decided the latter.

After the the meal, he excused himself, saying he'd had a long journey and would be up early.

'Good night, Monsieur, please let Madame Picard know if you require a packed lunch or if you will eat here,' Hélène said. 'While you are with us, please consider the château your home.'

'A pleasant man,' Hélène said when he left the room. 'But I fear one who is full of demons.'

8

Isabelle slept fitfully. James featured in all her dreams. His green eyes looking deeply into hers, his arms around her, holding her close. It was all so vivid, she fancied she could feel his kiss on her neck when she awoke and she put her hand over the spot, to try to recreate the sensation.

The sky was still crimson and orange when she finally gave up trying to sleep and got up.

The temporary repair that James had carried out the previous day had held during the storm and Hélène's bedroom was dry, although she suspected the canvas wouldn't hold for very long. Perhaps it would be a good idea to go and see Étienne and beg him to come and mend the roof.

She received letters from Flora and Madeleine regularly and things seemed to be going well at Maison Dubois, but it would be a relief to take Hélène to England and not to have to worry about the upkeep of the château.

The appearance of James had shaken her. In England she was well-respected as an independent business woman but here, she didn't seem to have a place. And of course, there were the memories . . .

She was dressing when she heard the crunch of gravel on the drive. At first, she thought it was James going out but she could tell it was a large vehicle and it was approaching the château, not leaving. Could it finally be Étienne?

She looked out of the bedroom window and saw that it was indeed Étienne in his van with ladders strapped to the roof. He pulled up outside the front door and climbed out to be greeted by James. The two men shook hands as if they knew each other and then she saw James take his wallet from his pocket, remove some Franc bills and place them in Étienne's hand.

The two men then turned to look up at the roof and a conversation followed with much pointing.

Isabelle rushed downstairs and by the time she'd reached the drive, Étienne had started to lean his ladders against the wall of the château and his son was unloading tools.

'Bonjour, Madame,' Étienne called to her and started climbing the ladder, whistling tunelessly.

When she went into the kitchen to get breakfast, James was there, sipping coffee.

'Étienne has come,' Madame Picard announced proudly, apparently forgetting that he was several weeks later than expected. 'More, Monsieur?' she asked, hovering at James' side, ready to refill his cup.

The corners of his mouth twitched as he caught Isabelle's eye. 'Thank you, Madame Picard, that's very kind of you.'

The housekeeper puffed out her chest and beamed with pleasure.

'How did you arrange it?' Isabelle asked.

'Me?' he said innocently, 'What makes you think it had anything to do with me?'

'I saw you and it looked like you were paying him,' she replied, sitting at the table.

'Ah, so you were spying on me?'

'Yes., no . . . I just happened to look out of the window,' she said, cheeks flaming. How did this man manage to make her feel like a schoolgirl?

'I went to see him yesterday afternoon and persuaded him that this should be a priority. Luckily, he saw things from my point of view.'

'It's such a relief to know that the roof will soon be watertight. I don't know how to thank you.'

'There *is* something you could do for me. There's a certain place I'd like to see again but I'm not sure I'm ready to go alone. Perhaps if you have time, you'll come with me?'

'Of course! Do you want to go

today?' Isabelle's heart skipped a beat. *Stop behaving like a silly girl!* She told herself and blushed at how eager she'd sounded. 'Although I was going to clean some of the other rooms now that the roof is being mended,' she forced herself to add.

'Of course. Well, if I help you clean this morning, perhaps we could go in the afternoon?'

Don't be so obvious, she thought, as she opened her mouth to agree. Instead, she pretended to consider his offer. 'Yes, all right, I think that might be possible.'

Madame Picard, who seemed to have fallen under James' spell insisted on packing a lunch for them once they'd changed, after cleaning several of the rooms. He helped Isabelle into the car and placed the lunch basket on the back seat.

'Is it far?' she asked, more to relieve the silence of the journey than because she really wanted to know.

'No,' he said, his eyes fixed firmly on

138

the road and his knuckles white as he gripped the steering wheel. She wanted to put her hand over his to comfort him but dared not. It was as though he wasn't really aware of her presence.

As he drove through a small village, he slowed, looking left and right as if searching for something. He shook his head sadly and sighed.

'The last time I saw this place, there was very little still standing. The church was damaged but the bell tower was still there. Other than that . . . ' He pulled up and applied the handbrake. 'There were just piles of bricks and rubble.'

He helped Isabelle out of the car.

Just like two people on a picnic, Isabelle thought, but she was certain this was not going to be like any other picnic she'd been on. For a start, he hadn't taken the basket and she didn't want to remind him of anything as prosaic as food when he appeared to be fighting with demons, as Hélène had described it.

He led the way along the road out of the village, heading into the countryside and every so often, he turned to stare at the horizon until he reached a thicket. 'This wasn't here,' he said stepping off the road and skirting round it. At last, he stopped with the trees behind him, staring intensely at the panorama. 'Can you hear that?' he asked.

Isabelle listened. Finally, she had to admit she couldn't hear anything out of the ordinary.

'Exactly,' he said with satisfaction and closed his eyes, 'I can hear birdsong, a grasshopper, and wind blowing through the leaves. Everything you'd expect to be in the country. No shells, no bullets, no screams . . . ' He tailed off.

Before Isabelle realised what she'd done, she'd slipped her hand into his. He turned and looked at her in surprise but rather than letting her hand drop, he held it as he gazed at the landscape. Finally, with a sigh, he released her fingers.

'I'm sorry,' she said, her cheeks glowing with embarrassment.

'Don't be,' he said. 'You being here is really helping. Since 1918, I've had such dreadful pictures in my mind, the scenes are as vivid as if I was still standing on the battlefield. For a long time, I didn't want to come back. It was irrational but I feared it'd be the same as when I left and I didn't want to reinforce the memories. But recently, I met someone who fought in Flanders and he said he'd gone back to find the graves of friends. He couldn't believe how the land had recovered. He said that in places, it was as if the fighting had never been and I wondered if I returned, could I replace the images in my head.'

He took a postcard-sized notebook out of his pocket and, opening it, he held it out for her to see. It was a drawing in bold, dark strokes of silhouetted soldiers bent over as they ran across No Man's Land strewn with

141

barbed wire. On the next page, was a soldier with helmet tipped back as he played the harmonica, crouched in a trench. Each page held a scene James had witnessed.

'When I left, the ground had been blown up repeatedly with shells and bombs and it was hard to believe anything would ever grow there again. There were no trees, just smashed and splintered trunks. I dreaded finding any traces of the fighting but now it's as if all that bloodshed and horror never took place.'

She turned to the next page. It was a portrait of a woman. Isabelle stared at it in disbelief.

'Ah,' he said, 'I hope you don't mind.'

'No, I was just a little surprised, that's all.'

She stared at the portrait of herself. The pencil strokes were much softer than the previous drawings and the likeness was excellent.

'You're a very skilled artist,' she said.

'But I didn't see you sketching me last night.'

'I have a photographic memory. I see something and then later, I simply draw what's in my mind. It's a blessing and a curse.'

She began to see how he must have been tormented since the war with such vivid images in his mind, and his current visit to the battlefields made sense.

'Will you go home and draw what you've seen today?' she asked.

'I don't know. It might be enough to have simply seen the fields transformed. There are a few places I'd still like to visit while I'm here, though. Shall I go and fetch the picnic basket?'

That evening, Isabelle spent a long-time pinning her hair up and choosing a dress. Would he draw her again once he was back in his room? A shiver of delight went through her and she scolded herself. James was beginning to penetrate the shell she'd carefully constructed around herself.

But he hasn't shown any interest in you at all, she reminded herself.

Except he took the time to draw you, a tiny voice inside replied.

He seems to draw lots of things. Remember the battle scenes?

It means nothing! Don't be so foolish!

★   ★   ★

Dinner had been a much lighter affair than the evening when James had first arrived. He was noticeably more relaxed and there was a great deal of laughter as they ate. Again, he excused himself early and Isabelle caught her breath, wondering if he was going to his bedroom to draw.

'Are you all right, Chérie?' Hélène asked. 'You seem to be rather flushed this evening. You're not coming down with anything, are you?'

Isabelle assured her mother she was fine and went to bed. She walked as slowly as she could when she passed

James's bedroom. There was a beam of light under the door but no sound and she knew that if he hadn't drawn her tonight, she would be very disappointed. More disappointed than she had a right to be.

At dinner, they'd discussed Étienne's progress and apparently he'd made a good start. In a few more weeks, if he kept working at the same rate, it would be done; she and Maman could go back to England and she would put these ridiculous thoughts behind her. She'd step back into her role as an independent business woman and this silly schoolgirl behaviour would be something she would merely remember with embarrassment.

*   *   *

The following morning, Isabelle was woken by the sound of a vehicle on the drive. For a second, she thought it was Étienne arriving early, until she realised it was leaving, not arriving. Leaping from bed, she was just in time to see the tail of a car turn on to the road before it was gone. Disappointment swept over her. The previous evening, James hadn't mentioned his plans for today. A sudden disturbing thought came to her that perhaps he had left.

She was wide awake so she got ready and went down to breakfast. Madame Picard wouldn't arrive with fresh bread for a while, so Isabelle poured herself a cup of coffee and forced herself to plan her day. She would clean more rooms and perhaps tackle the cellar. That would take her mind off James. If only she knew where he was.

It occurred to her that if she were to knock at his bedroom and there was no reply, she would be able to see if his suitcase was still there. If it had gone, she would know that he'd decided to leave for some reason.

But suppose she'd been mistaken and it hadn't been James' car? Suppose he was still asleep? Well, she could simply say she was checking because someone may have stolen his car.

With her story straight, she crept back upstairs and tapped gently on James's door. There was no reply and after tapping gently again, she opened the door. His bed was unmade but he wasn't there, and his suitcase still stood in the corner. *At least he intends to return*, she thought with more relief than she knew she had the right to feel.

On the desk was a sketch book. It wasn't the postcard-sized book he'd shown her yesterday, but much larger, and several pencils lay nearby.

Don't touch it! she warned herself as she crept towards it, but she knew she wasn't going to be able to stop herself. The book was open at the page where James had last been drawing and she gasped when she saw the portrait he'd drawn.

It was definitely her — and so realistic, it could have been a photograph. He'd faithfully reproduced exactly how she'd looked last night.

Clattering from downstairs in the kitchen announced that Madame Picard had arrived. Isabelle jumped away from the sketch book guiltily then retraced her footsteps out of his bedroom.

When she arrived in the kitchen, Madame Picard hastily tied her apron strings, cut a few slices off a loaf of bread and placed them on a plate for Isabelle. There was a knock at the back door and Isabelle looked up, hoping it was James — but it was Étienne. He entered with his hat in his hands, an anxious frown furrowing his brow.

'Ah, Madame, I was hoping to see you or your mother.' He cleared his throat and twisted the hat in his hands.

'Get on with it!' said Madame Picard.

'Well, it's just that I'm afraid I won't be able to finish the roof as quickly as I said.'

'Why not?'

'It's my supplier,' he said. 'Timber has risen in price and he's finding it hard to get hold of what I need. If he does manage to get any, it will double the price of the job.'

'Double the price?' Isabelle had brought plenty money but she wouldn't be able to pay twice as much as Étienne had first asked for. She would have to write to Flora to ask her to send more. 'If I can find the money, how much longer will it take?'

'Oh, er . . . ' Étienne looked down at his hat, as if unable to meet her gaze. 'It could be months.'

'Months?' Isabelle couldn't believe it. She couldn't stay here for months! Not without Madeleine. She was so shocked, she didn't hear James enter the kitchen.

'But, Monsieur Picard,' he asked, 'how long would it take if you had the right timber?'

'Oh, er,' Étienne looked like a trapped animal. 'A few weeks, like I said in the beginning. But I don't have the right timber. Or the correct tiles.'

'Let me know what you need,' said

James. 'I have contacts, I'll see if I can find another supplier. Why don't you carry on working with what you have? I'll see what I can find out today.'

Étienne's mouth opened and closed several times but no sound came out. Finally, he nodded and went back outside.

'That was rather strange,' said Isabelle.

James nodded. 'I went into Montplessis earlier to send a telegram to my boss and I saw Étienne talking to someone. I don't think he was a timber merchant — he was dressed in a suit. The reason I noticed was that as the man spoke, he kept poking Étienne in the chest with a finger and it crossed my mind that Étienne might punch him but he just stood there taking it.'

'Oh!' Madame Picard let out a soft sound like a punctured tyre, 'It must be Monsieur Charbonel. Étienne owes him money.'

'It makes sense,' said Isabelle. 'The delightful Monsieur Charbonel came

150

here shortly a few weeks ago and offered to buy Château Bellevais and the estate. As it's in such a dilapidated condition, he barely offered us anything at all and Maman turned him down. He was not happy. Perhaps he thinks if we can't mend the roof, we'll sell. Can you get Étienne what he needs?'

'Possibly.' James was hesitant. 'I'll make a few telephone calls and find out.'

'Don't go to Montplessis,' said Madame Picard. 'If you telephone from there, Monsieur Charbonel will know. He makes it his business to keep people in his debt and I've heard the postmistress owes him money. Go to Beauvais, Monsieur. Telephone from there.'

★   ★   ★

Isabelle turned to wave to her mother who was waiting at the front door. Hélène had decided to stay at home as she still got out of breath easily and didn't want to risk delaying James in finding a new timber supplier. With a stab of guilt, Isabelle realised she was glad her mother had wanted to stay because it was so wonderful to be driving along the lanes with James and to have the prospect of an afternoon with him.

True, he'd be telephoning contacts and suppliers, and while he did that, she would be shopping for samples of fabrics and trimmings to take home, but to be sitting within reach of him was heady stuff. That feeling she had experienced all those years ago with Tom was reasserting itself. She had entered a make-believe world in which she and James existed in complete isolation. Whatever they did wouldn't affect anyone outside the carefully constructed bubble, and no one could affect them.

Yet 'make-believe' was the part she had to focus on. It was completely in her imagination and that was where it must stay, since James had behaved like a perfect gentleman.

Later she arrived at the bar where she'd arranged to meet James, a large parcel under her arm. He was seated at one of the busy tables and he waved to attract her attention, then smiled at her with such pleasure that her heart leapt.

'I've got a new supplier — and guess what?' he asked, relieving her of the parcel. 'It's cheaper than you were originally paying.'

The realisation that his delight hadn't been in seeing her but in the news that he had to give her brought her back to the present with a jolt.

'Wonderful,' she said, hoping that she sounded suitably enthusiastic, and then added, 'Thank you so much, James, you've been a real help. Maman will be so relieved.'

After lunch, they strolled through the colourful, bustling market and stopped to buy peaches at a fruit stall. As they made their way back to the car, they left the marketplace and turned down a narrow street lined with shops.

'Are you all right, Isabelle? You've gone white.'

'Yes, I'm fine, thanks,' she said quickly.

This was the road where she'd picked up Tom's photographs from the studio. To her relief, it was now a florist with ranks of bright flowers outside. She dared not stop and look in case James asked why she was taking so much interest. Tom was firmly in her past. Just a fleeting moment and she didn't want James to know. She didn't want his opinion of her — whatever that was — to change because of one evening in her youth.

But what about Madeleine? You still haven't even mentioned you have a daughter.

But why should that interest James? He was merely a guest about whom she was spinning an imaginary love story, and as he would never know what was in her imagination, he need not know about Madeleine.

'So, what d'you think?' he asked.

'Sorry?' She'd been lost in her thoughts.

'Is there anywhere nice to stop on the way back home?'

'There's a lake. It's a bit out of the way but not too far. Why?'

He'd stopped outside a patisserie and pointed at the mouth-watering cakes and pastries.

'We could buy some and eat them on the way home. We can take something for Madame Rousseau as well.'

As they walked from the car to the edge of the lake, Isabelle stumbled slightly; her heels were too high to walk easily over such rough ground and he held her elbow to steady her. She thrilled at the touch of his palm against her bare arm.

Choosing a grassy spot, he laid out a travel rug and suggested they sit. There was so much she wanted to ask him as they sat watching the ducks glide through the expanse of water.

Had his idea to visit battlefields and to exorcise the memories worked

— would he be leaving soon? Why was he so polite and yet so distant? Why had he drawn her portrait?

Instead, she asked him about the timber and tiles he'd ordered for the roof. 'There's one thing that worries me,' she said. 'What do you think Monsieur Charbonel might do when he finds we have supplies from elsewhere? He seems to have some sort of hold over Étienne, so what happens if he stops him working for us?'

'Surely once he sees you've taken the initiative and that you're determined, he'll leave you alone? To be on the safe side, when the supplier delivers tomorrow, we'll ask him to put everything out of sight in the stable yard at the back of the château. It won't be long before Étienne has finished the roof at the front of the building and once he's working on the back, he won't be visible from the drive. So if your charming Monsieur Charbonel passes, he won't see a thing.'

He took out his small sketch book

and started to draw the lake with confident strokes.

'What do you think you'll do with the château?' he asked.

She lay back on the rug, hands under her head.

'I don't really know. Perhaps one day Maman will agree to sell it, but definitely not to Monsieur Charbonel. She's not well enough yet to make decisions like that but hopefully once we get to England and she recovers, we'll have a chance to think about it. I don't see how I can run Maison Dubois *and* look after the château.'

After a while, he tore a page out of his sketch book and handed it to her. On one side was a sketch of the lake and on the other, was a portrait of her lying back on the rug.

'I hope you don't mind,' he said, 'But you look so beautiful lying there, I couldn't resist . . . '

She sat up, suddenly shy — exposed almost, as if he'd seen more of her than she'd known she was showing, as though an act of intimacy had occurred without him even touching her.

'Do you mind?' he asked, leaning down and brushing her cheek with his finger. 'If you do, tell me and I'll stop. It's just that I can't get you out of my mind . . .'

'No.' She placed her hand over his and held his warm palm to her cheek. 'I don't mind at all.'

Gently, he pulled her towards him, his mouth seeking hers, and when their lips touched, she wondered if she was going to faint.

She barely remembered Tom's feverish kisses and there had only been one or two of the men who she went out with in Guildford, whom she'd allowed to kiss her. It had meant nothing. She marvelled that she had lived for over thirty years but never felt anything like this before.

The sensation of his hand at the nape of her neck sent shivers of delight running through her body and his lips moved down her throat, towards her shoulders. She let her head drop back and closed her eyes as he reached the hollow at the base of her throat, her breath coming in short gasps. He undid the top button of her blouse and planted tiny kisses on her chest until he reached the next button, then undid that.

A shrill whistle cut through the peace of the river, sending a flock of birds squawking into the air, breaking the spell that bound them and they sprang apart.

'Bruno!' a man shouted as a Labrador ran up to the couple on the rug, its tongue lolling out of its mouth as it bounded towards them.

'Bruno! Come here!' the man shouted again and the dog turned and ran towards him.

If the man saw Isabelle and James on the rug, he took no notice and wandered off back into the woods, followed by his dog.

James looked at Isabelle with concern, as if trying to judge her mood.

She was embarrassed because she knew that had the man arrived a few minutes later or indeed, hadn't announced himself by calling his dog, she would have been behaving in public in what would be considered an inappropriate manner. But strangely, she wasn't as bothered as she would have thought.

James' touch had seemed so right. It had incited a reaction that was completely new and one she regretted had stopped. It suddenly occurred to her that if James apologised, she would be extremely hurt.

When she'd spent the night with Tom, he'd said he was sorry when he realised what he'd done and it had spoiled the pleasure she'd experienced. She wasn't sorry.

'Are you upset?' he asked, holding her by the shoulders and trying to make her meet his gaze.

'I will be, if you tell me you're sorry for what almost happened just then.'

'How could I be sorry for doing what I've wanted to do since I first laid eyes on you?' He placed a finger under her chin and lifted her head so she was looking directly at him. 'Unless you hadn't wanted to, but I thought you were happy too.'

'I was . . . I am,' she said. 'I just don't want you to think I'm a mistake. An error of judgement.'

'Isabelle, I've never been as happy as I have these last few days while I've been with you.' He kissed her tenderly, then pulled her to her feet. 'But the location left a lot to be desired. The next time I kiss you, we'll be alone,' he said, gently running his fingertip over her bottom lip.

★　★　★

Hélène knew something had changed as soon as Isabelle and James returned from Beauvais and she was certain it had nothing to do with his success in finding a new source for roofing materials.

During dinner, Hélène watched the

smouldering glances and secret smiles with alarm. It was wonderful to see her daughter so happy but as soon as the roof was mended, they would be packing up to go to England — and James worked in France. A relationship was out of the question.

She had longed for Isabelle to find someone to make her as happy as she had been with her darling Philippe, someone who made Isabelle feel whole. But this development was new, and she doubted it would survive if the couple lived in different countries. Isabelle would have to return to Maison Dubois — if only to sell it and return to France, but it wouldn't be as simple as that.

There was Madeleine to think of and unless Isabelle had told James about her daughter today, she was fairly certain he knew nothing about her. Hélène had noted how Isabelle had avoided any mention of Madeleine when talking about her life in England. She didn't blame her — after all, until today, James had simply been a guest in their home and no one had owed him an explanation. But now Hélène suspected that despite the young couple's obvious delight in each other, they were both heading towards heartache.

'Isabelle and I can't thank you enough for finding us an alternative supplier for our roofing materials, James,' she said as she poured wine into his glass. 'I don't know what we'd have done if Monsieur Charbonel had delayed the repairs. Isabelle has spent enough time here looking after me and she needs to return to her business and her . . . commitments as soon as possible.'

She busied herself pouring wine for Isabelle and pretended not to see the glance the young couple exchanged.

'And I expect you're keen to get back to your life in Caen. It's a sad fact that holidays always come to an end and real life takes over.'

'I'm not in a great rush to finish my holiday,' James said, 'But you are, of course, correct. Holidays always come to an end.'

Hélène pushed the food around her plate and noted that neither James nor Isabelle ate much.

She couldn't imagine how they were both feeling, and the fact that her words had caused them both pain weighed heavily on her conscience. But it was a mother's duty to protect her child. This budding relationship was doomed and the sooner they both saw there was no future for them together, the less misery they'd endure.

Hélène proposed they all retire early and suggested that Isabelle help her in the morning to start wrapping up and storing the things they were leaving in the château and packing up those they were going to take to Guildford.

'Now the end is in sight for the roof repairs, we need to set a date for our journey to England.'

Isabelle nodded, 'Yes, of course, Maman,' she said but the light had gone out in her eyes and her voice was lifeless. Hélène wanted to weep.

⋆   ⋆   ⋆

Isabelle slept fitfully. She knew what her mother was doing and accepted she was right, but it hurt nevertheless.

There must be a way for her and James to be together — at least until they found out if there really was any substance to the attraction they felt for each other. The best plan she could think of involved visiting each other as often as they could, but how often would she be able to get away from Maison Dubois to go to France? And how often would he be able to visit her in Guildford? The alternative was to part now — but she couldn't contemplate such a loss.

It was still dark when she got out of bed. The crunch of gravel told her someone was walking down the drive to the road and she knew it was James. Leaping from bed, she could see a dark figure carrying a bag on his back and guessed he was going on a long walk. Perhaps he needed to clear his head and think about the future.

She went down to the deserted kitchen and made coffee. It would be several hours before Madame Picard arrived or Maman came down for breakfast and she sat miserably at the long, wooden table, cradling a cup of coffee and staring out of the window at the grey dawn.

Later, she helped Hélène to wrap up the paintings and priceless ornaments which would be placed in the cellar, with the help of Madame Picard, whose comments showed that she assumed the silent gloom to be a result of Hélène's sadness at leaving her home and Isabelle's reluctance to return to England.

'Who on earth would leave France to go to England, of all places?' she asked with a shrug.

Isabelle was content to let Madame Picard chatter about the shortcomings of England — at least it filled what would otherwise have been a gloomy atmosphere. She understood why her mother had spoken as she had, but it wasn't a message she'd wanted to hear.

Stop being so childish! she told herself. There wasn't any point in blaming her mother for her circumstances. It wasn't her fault the man she was falling for lived in a different country. It was simply another example of life holding out something tempting and then snatching it away.

Isabelle watched her mother wrap a framed photograph of her father in soft fabric, lingering before she drew the edges of the material over him. Hélène's head was bowed and Isabelle knew she was hiding tears. How sad Maman must be at finally leaving the château that held so many memories of her husband and their life together.

How could she have failed to realise how hard this would be for Maman? Isabelle rose and placed her arm round her mother's shoulder.

'If you'd like to rest a while, Maman, I could finish this.'

Hélène shook her head, 'Thank you, Chérie, but I can manage. I'm saying goodbye to your father as I do this . . . ' Her voice caught and Isabelle kissed the top of her head.

Her mother had been trying to save her the pain of separation from James before she became too attached. But Isabelle realised it was too late — she had already fallen for him.

9

The entire day had passed in silent thoughtfulness and the evening meal was no different. James had not returned by the time the two women retired for the night and if it hadn't been for the fact that his car was still parked near the stable and his suitcase still in his bedroom, Isabelle would have thought he'd gone.

Making the excuse to Hélène that she would take a small snack to his bedroom for when he returned, she carried the tray inside and placed it on the table, but dared not stay long because she knew the creaking floorboards would betray where she was. She left his door open to minimise the noise it would make when he returned . . . if he returned. *Perhaps he's found somewhere else to stay the night*, she thought with a jolt of disappointment.

She lay awake for hours, hearing the grandfather clock in the hall chime one, two and three o'clock, but must have fallen asleep soon after because she woke with a start just as the sun began to glow in the east. Her eyes were swollen and gritty but she knew she wouldn't sleep any longer. She hadn't heard James return and unless he'd crept back to his room during the short time she'd been asleep, he wasn't home.

She tiptoed to the door and opened it centimetre by centimetre. Finally in the hall, she avoided the floorboards which creaked the most and made her way past Hélène's room. The door to James's bedroom was still open as she'd left it the previous night. Her stomach lurched with disappointment at the sight of the empty room and tidy bed. She was tempted to go back to bed, crawl inside and pull the covers over her head. What was there to get up for now? But she knew it would upset Hélène — after all, it was she who had tried to protect her. It would hurt her more if Isabelle demonstrated her sadness. The move to England wasn't going to be easy for Hélène, so she ought to comfort her mother, not upset her.

She hurried down to the kitchen to make a cup of strong coffee to jolt her to wakefulness, then she would get ready and start carrying some of the boxes that she had packed the previous day, into the wine cellar.

Madame Picard would not arrive for another hour and Hélène didn't rise until the housekeeper took her a cup of coffee in bed, so Isabelle expected the kitchen to be empty.

James looked up in surprise as she opened the door. He was seated at the long kitchen table, his arms crossed on the table in front of him, as if he was deep in thought.

'Isabelle!' He leapt to his feet and walked towards her.

She froze in the doorway and crossed her arms over her chest, aware that she was only wearing a thin nightdress.

'I'm so glad you came down! I need to talk to you — on your own,' he said, taking her hands and drawing her towards him. 'I know we haven't known each other long and it's too soon to discuss a future together, but as your mother pointed out last night, time is running out for us and if I don't say anything now, it might be too late. I can't stop thinking about you, Isabelle. When you're not there, I long to be with you — to hold you. I can't bear to be away from you ... ' He stared deeply into her eyes, waiting for her response.

'Oh, James, I feel the same way, but how can we be together? I can't stay in France.'

'I know. So, I telephoned my boss Michel, today and asked if I could take time off. I want to go to England to be near you, so we can give our feelings a chance to grow. But if you don't feel the same way ... '

'You'd come to England ... for me?'

'I'd go anywhere to be with you, Isabelle.'

She threw her arms round his neck.

'And what did Michel say?' she asked, looking up at him.

'He wasn't very happy to begin with because he's just taken on a new job, so I'll have to go back to Caen and help with that before I leave for England. But in the end, we even discussed me opening up a new office for him in London.'

'So we can be together?' Isabelle could hardly believe it.

'If you want us to be.'

'Yes! Oh yes!'

He kissed her gently on the forehead, then cupping her face in his hands, he brushed her lips with his, sending Shockwaves of pleasure through her. His kisses became more urgent and she clung to him, the world receding as if they were the only two beings who existed. As his hands stroked her shoulders, she knew the nightdress was slipping but the feelings of pleasure that radiated through her as he caressed her skin engulfed her completely. Undoing the buttons of his shirt, she felt his naked skin against hers.

The rattle of the door handle brought them both back to the present. The wicker basket creaked as Madame Picard transferred it to the other arm and tried the broken door handle again. By the time she'd succeeded, Isabelle and James were running stealthily upstairs hand-in-hand, trying to suppress laughter at almost being caught.

James kissed her again before going into his bedroom. 'When shall we tell your mother?'

'As soon as she's up.'

Isabelle crept back to her bedroom. She peered into the mirror and her eyes, which had been swollen and gritty when she woke, now sparkled.

James wanted to be with her! He was willing to give up his life in France for her. Would he still feel the same about her in England? And what would he think when she told him about Madeleine?

The sparkle in her eyes dimmed slightly as she wondered how he would react to the revelation.

It would have been better if she'd told him when he'd first suggested he go to England with her, but their kisses had taken over common sense. She would tell him about Madeleine before they told Hélène. Then he would have the opportunity to change his mind if he wanted, without her mother knowing anything about the plans.

As soon as Isabelle was ready, she rushed downstairs to find James. She would ask him to go for a walk and tell him about Madeleine before Maman got up. He was waiting for her, his face lighting up as she entered — but Madame Picard had just poured him some coffee and before he could finish it, Hélène came into the kitchen.

* * *

'Chérie! I am so sorry, I had no idea you hadn't told him about Madeleine. If only I'd known!'

Hélène held her hands to her face in horror.

'I was going to tell him this morning, Maman. Do you think I should follow him?'

'I don't know, Chérie. He seemed very hurt. Perhaps it's better to leave him for a while . . . '

Isabelle bit her lower lip, reliving the last five minutes when James had told Hélène of his plans to move to England. She'd said she was thrilled and that she was certain he'd love Madeleine and she, in turn, would love him.

'Who is Madeleine?' he'd asked.

When Isabelle had explained, he'd said coldly, 'And it didn't occur to you to mention your daughter before now?' Then he turned and walked out of the kitchen to the stables.

His look of incomprehension and betrayal haunted her. She waited until she could bear it no longer and left the château in search of him.

If only she'd had a chance to explain! He might not have welcomed the news that she had a daughter but at least she'd have had an opportunity to put her side of the story. Now, it looked as if she hadn't intended to tell him at all.

Isabelle found him down by the lake sitting on a log. His elbows rested on his knees as he stared fixedly into the water. She sat down next to him silently, not sure how he would receive her.

'I'm so sorry, James. I was going to tell you this morning. I swear it was not my intention to deceive you.'

He turned his gaze from the water and looked at her, hurt and betrayal evident in his eyes.

'I wouldn't have minded,' he said, 'but I can't stand dishonesty. How can I trust you now?'

'I had no idea I would fall for you, James. At first, you were just a guest in our house, a stranger. Should I have told you then? I've grown used to hiding the fact that Madeleine is illegitimate — for her sake more than mine. I made one mistake a long time ago. Now society demands Madeleine and I both pay for it forever. I can accept *my* punishment but it's not fair *she* should suffer. So I took her father's name when I arrived in England, allowed people to assume I was a war widow. I am not proud of that, James, but I could see no other way to protect my daughter.' Isabelle faltered, fighting back tears. 'Even when it was clear we were becoming attracted to each other, I did not expect us to have a future. I thought we would never see each other again. Should I have told you then?'

Still, he said nothing.

'There never seemed to be a right time to tell you, James — not until this morning, and then Maman beat me to it.'

They sat at either end of the log, both staring ahead into the water. Finally, she stood. He obviously hadn't forgiven her. It was over before it had really begun. She turned to go.

'Is there anything else you haven't told me?'

'I'll tell you everything you want to know,' she said, 'I'm not used to sharing, I've been on my own for so long, but I'll tell you about a naive girl who thought she had a situation under control when she tried to comfort a battle-weary soldier. I'll tell you about the magical fairy tale life she imagined she would one day live, until she finally discovered the truth. And then I'll tell you how she suppressed her emotions and closed her eyes to the possibility that magic might exist.'

She swallowed hard and began the sorry tale of her life. It would be painful to display her life for his scrutiny, but what did she have to lose . . . ?

*   *   *

'Grâce à Dieu!' said Madame Picard.

She was helping Hélène wrap the paintings which they'd removed from the walls of her bedroom, but at every opportunity the two women would glance out of one of the windows, searching for a sign of Isabelle or James.

Now, the housekeeper had spotted them both returning hand in hand.

Hélène rushed to her side. 'Yes indeed, thanks be to God,' she said with relief.

'Monsieur Hart is a fine man,' declared Madame Picard. 'And anyone can see those two people are made for each other.'

Hélène was too emotional to reply. For years she had prayed her daughter would find someone special who would be able to penetrate the thick wall she'd built around herself. How dreadful it would have been if Isabelle met him and then lost him because of her ill-timed words.

* * *

That night at dinner, Isabelle laid the table, setting her place next to James rather than her usual seat next to Hélène. It was as if, finding him again, she wasn't going to let him far from her side. Hélène noted with pleasure that at every opportunity their hands touched and as they looked at each other, their faces radiated happiness.

James had to return to Caen to work on the new architectural assignment Michel had taken on. He would leave early in the morning so he could start work on the project and finish it as soon as possible, then he would let Isabelle know when he would be free to leave for London. If it was before the women left France, he would join them on their journey, if not, he would follow them to England later.

That night, Isabelle lay awake, too excited to sleep. When Hélène had announced she was going to bed, she and James had kissed passionately but she had pulled away and asked if he would mind waiting until they were in England.

'I've made too many mistakes in my

life to risk getting this wrong,' she whispered, 'Can we get to know each other properly? And then . . . '

He'd seemed disappointed but immediately helped her straighten her dress, gently held her long hair back as she replaced the pearl combs, and then kissed her tenderly.

'Until England,' he said, tracing her cheek with a fingertip, 'And then the rest of our lives.'

She must have fallen deeply asleep finally because when she awoke, there was a sheet of paper poked under her door, although she hadn't heard anyone approach her room along the creaky floorboards of the corridor.

It was a sketch of Isabelle wearing the pearl necklace she'd worn the previous evening, but rather than a likeness of her while they'd eaten dinner, her hair pinned up with pearl combs and her black dress with its V-neck and short, lacy cap sleeves, he hadn't drawn the dress at all — just her bare shoulders over which were tendrils of hair that had escaped from the combs. Her head was thrown back and her lips parted as if she was waiting for his kiss. This was obviously what he remembered from last night and she blushed deeply as the image stimulated the sensations she'd felt herself.

Holding the portrait to her chest, she rushed to the window to see if his car had gone, knowing that if he'd left her this drawing, he had indeed left for Caen.

10

Monsieur Charbonel greeted the post-mistress, 'Ah, bonjour, Madame. And how is young Pierre today? Better, I trust?'

'Not really, he's still very poorly, but thank you for asking, Monsieur Charbonel. And thank you so much for paying for our trip to Paris. The doctors were really kind.'

'Can't they do anything for him?

'They've prescribed medicines, but . . . '

'Yes?'

'I can't afford them.'

'I see.'

'They say I should take him away, somewhere like the Alps where the air is clean, but . . . '

'If it's a question of money, I'm sure I could find my way clear to lending you some more.'

'Thank you, Monsieur but I cannot pay what you lent me already'

'A gift then.'

Henriette Girardot clasped her hands together, 'A gift? You would *give* me the money?'

'It would be my pleasure to help, Madame.'

'Oh, Monsieur, that would be too kind!'

He patted her hand. 'Don't mention it, Madame . . . Oh, and by the way, I have a little favour to ask of you . . . '

Her face was now guarded and she withdrew her hand from beneath his.

'I simply want to know if you receive a telegram from a Monsieur James Hart.'

'But I'm not supposed to . . . '

'Oh, come now, Madame. Étienne Picard is doing some repairs at the château and he tells me Madame Rousseau is thinking of engaging an architect. I've heard some bad reports about Monsieur Hart's work and it would only be fair to warn Madame

Rousseau and her daughter. I won't bother them unless Monsieur Hart tries to contact them. All I need is for you to telephone me if you receive any messages from him and hold on to them for me. Do you think you can do that for me?' he asked, taking his bulging wallet from his pocket and opening it to reveal a large number of bank notes. He took a few out and laid them on the counter. 'Madame?'

Still, she hesitated.

'I'm trying to prevent Madame Rousseau from making a grave mistake and the best way to do that is to stop all communication between them. You do understand, don't you, Madame?'

Henriette placed her hand over the notes and slid them close, slipping them into her pocket.

'You can rely on me, Monsieur.'

Several hours later, Monsieur Charbonel came to the back of the post office and handed over more cash. Henriette looked right and left and before taking the money and then passing him the telegram.

He walked back to his car and, once inside, he tore the telegram into pieces.

One day, the château would be his. The Rousseau woman had no idea about looking after such a large and ancient building. She neither had the funds nor the experience. With the young architect out of the picture, she would struggle to maintain the building and one day, perhaps with some help from Étienne, he would persuade her to sell. At a price that was beneficial to him.

11

It had been three days since James left for Caen and there had been no word despite his promises to contact her as soon as he knew how long it would take him to complete the project that Michel had taken on.

'Go into Montplessis and telephone him, Chérie. He's probably thrown himself into his work so he can be with you.'

Doubt gnawed at Isabelle.

Suppose he'd had second thoughts once he'd got back to normal life? Perhaps the prospect of meeting Madeleine was too daunting. They had known each other for such a short time, and she realised she didn't know much about him at all.

He'd never mentioned Michel's surname nor the name of the architectural company, so it would be difficult to find the telephone number. And even if she had it, she wasn't sure she would have telephoned him. If he had changed his mind, she didn't want to hear it from his lips. She might be tormented by doubts but at least, she still had hope that he'd contact her.

Now too, she had other things on her mind. A letter from England had arrived on the day James left for Normandy.

Apparently, since she'd been in France, Hugh Mansfield had been making a nuisance of himself. Madeleine hadn't gone into detail but whatever had happened had been enough for her to suggest they move away from Guildford. The tone of the letter had been light-hearted, but reading between the lines, Isabelle knew that something serious had happened.

She didn't bother Hélène with her worries. They'd both soon be in England and would undoubtedly find out exactly what had happened.

In the meantime, she wrote to say that she and Hélène would be in France for a few more weeks while the roof repairs were finished, but she was happy for Flora and Madeleine to look for suitable new premises if they thought it best to move.

★   ★   ★

In Caen, James was disappointed when he saw the size of the contract that Michel had won. It was a project for a grand new building on the outskirts of the city, which ordinarily would have thrilled him, but now it was merely an obstacle to him leaving and being with Isabelle.

He had promised he wouldn't leave until Michel could find a replacement, but that meant he couldn't give Isabelle a definite date when he could join her. One thing was for sure, it wouldn't be before they left France. He would work until he dropped if necessary and then join her in England.

He sent a telegram telling her that he'd see her in England and asking her to send the address of her home in Guildford.

Then he immersed himself in meetings, surveys, designs and drawings.

12

Madeleine rushed into the shop and waved her letter at Flora. 'Look, Maman and Mémé are coming home in two weeks! And she says she's happy for us to move. If we find somewhere suitable she'll sign all the legal papers when she gets here.'

Flora sighed. 'It's a shame she has to come home to such unpleasantness. You didn't tell her what happened, did you?'

'No, I told you I wouldn't. I just said Hugh had been making a nuisance of himself.'

That was an understatement!

Madeleine usually wrote last thing at night, despite having gritty, tired eyes after hours of sewing or drawing designs. Her letters were full of amusing tales about people that Isabelle knew ... Mrs Brownlee had complained that the dress she'd made several months ago was too small, despite it fitting when she'd bought it; the lady whose wedding dress Isabelle had made was now expecting a baby; and Flora had turned down another invitation to the cinema.

At first, she'd told her mother about Hugh Mansfield coming in each day to enquire when Isabelle would return, but lately he'd been making her slightly ill at ease and she thought it best not to worry her mother about something she couldn't quite define.

He was often seen sitting in the café opposite, watching the shop. However, it was his expression when he spoke to her that was alarming. She hadn't told anyone, not even Flora, but when he mentioned Isabelle's name, something wild flashed in his eyes and there was a certain intensity in his manner. He spoke about Isabelle as though they were close friends — intimate, almost. Madeleine knew this wasn't true but no one else had remarked on his behaviour so she kept it to herself.

Recently, he'd demanded she give him Isabelle's address and the more she refused, the more insistent he became. That afternoon when she was returning from the grocer's, he'd intercepted her and asked again when Isabelle would be home.

'She'll be very angry when she knows you've refused to give me her address. I'm an old friend.'

'I think I know my mother better than you!'

'Come now. I only want to send her a card. How can that be wrong?'

He seemed obsessed with her mother and she wondered whether he might go to France to find her — something she knew Isabelle wouldn't like.

'Leave a card with me and I'll post it the next time I write.'

He'd barged past her then and walked off. But later that evening as she was locking up, he returned and pushed into the shop. Flora was upstairs preparing dinner and the other girls had left for the day.

'Good evening.' He raised his hat and stumbled sideways, knocking her backwards, his breath heavy with alcohol.

'Where'sh Ishabelle? I wanna see Ishabelle . . . '

'She's not here, Mr Mansfield. I'm sorry but I have to close up the shop. Perhaps you'd come back tomorrow.'

'Will she be here tomorrow? I missh her.'

'No, Mr Mansfield. She's looking after my grandmother in France.'

'Oh yesh. Well, when will she be back? I have to see her. I have to see my Ishabelle . . . '

'I'm sorry, I don't know when she'll be back.'

'But I need her.'

'I think that what you need, Mr Mansfield is to go home and sober up. My mother wouldn't wish to see you in this state even if she was here.'

'No!' he said grabbing her wrist, 'You don't undershtand. I love Ishabelle!'

Madeleine's irritation began to turn to fear. Despite his unsteadiness, his grip was tight and she knew no one would hear her if she shouted. She took the opportunity to step away from him as he ran his hands through his dishevelled hair.

'Mr Mansfield, I really need to lock up, so perhaps you could call tomorrow?' she asked in as calm a voice as she could muster.

'Tomorrow? I can't wait until tomorrow!' He lunged, grasping her jaw in one hand and forcing her back against the wall. 'I want you to put in a good word for me. Tell her I love her.'

Madeleine could neither open her mouth to speak nor move her head to nod.

'Mr Mansfield, how can we help you?' It was Flora at the stairs leading to their apartment.

Hugh swung round in surprise, his hand dropping from Madeleine's face. He began to sob. 'I need her, I need Ishabelle.'

'Yes, I quite understand,' said Flora soothingly, 'But now, it's time for you to go.' She shepherded him towards the door. 'Isabelle wouldn't want to see you like this.'

'No, I shpose not . . . '

'Why not come back tomorrow. We'll probably have news from France.'

'Yesh. Yesh, I will.' He stumbled into the street.

With trembling hands, Flora closed the door and turned the key, then slid both bolts into place.

'Darling! Are you all right?'

Madeleine nodded, her eyes glistening with tears as she massaged her bruised jaw.

'Yes, I'm fine — just a little shaken — but thank goodness you came. I'm so angry with myself for not doing something. He was so unsteady, I'm sure if I'd pushed him, I could have got away.'

'Darling, don't be hard on yourself. It's easy to be wise after the event. When I was looking for Peter in Paris, I was often in danger and when I thought about it afterwards, I could see how I should have reacted. It took a while before I learned to anticipate and handle difficult situations. We'll call Constable Preston tomorrow. He won't let Mr Hugh Mansfield bother us again.'

Madeleine lay awake for hours that night. Despite Flora's words, they both knew it would take more than bumbling Constable Preston to keep Hugh away. If only they could all move to France . . . but she knew Maman relied on the money from the business. She had to keep the shop open. But after tonight's experience, she'd lost all enthusiasm for Maison Dubois.

You're just feeling tired and vulnerable, she told herself, but despite having lived most of her life in Guildford, she suddenly felt she didn't belong. With Aunt Dorothy and Maman gone, it seemed as though she had no ties to it.

And now there was Hugh Mansfield. She'd seen him sitting in the café opposite the shop, watching them. He'd appeared quite absurd before but now she'd seen the extent of his obsession with Maman . . .

The following day, Madeleine suggested to Flora that they sell the shop and buy another in Paris so they could be near Isabelle. If they went to France, Hélène could stay in her own home which they would be able to renovate. But Flora wasn't keen on returning to a city that held so many unhappy memories, and Madeleine knew she wouldn't be able to manage on her own.

Perhaps Flora would agree to move to London. They wouldn't be able to afford property in the West End, but perhaps the East End? She remembered her trip to Stepney to look for her half-sister, Joanna. She'd noticed many dress shops there — perhaps too many to make it sensible to open another. Anyway, she'd also seen the grimy tenement blocks festooned with heavily laden washing lines. Beneath the flapping clothes, swarms of barefoot children played. The families crammed into the tenements didn't look as though they could afford even second-hand clothes, certainly not the exclusive fashions she and Flora created.

She wondered yet again what had happened to Joanna and what it would have been like had she found her . . . and then, she had it.

What about Essex? Of course, Joanna may not have stayed there but it might be worth a trip to Laindon to find out. It might turn out to be the perfect place to open Maison Dubois — if she could convince Flora to go with her.

⋆　⋆　⋆

It was Flora who was the one to make the final decision to move to Laindon High Street. She'd been sceptical at first.

'Laindon? Never heard of it. Some sleepy backwater in the middle of the Essex countryside. Who'd want to buy our clothes there?'

Madeleine was half-convinced she might be right but she was also keen to see the town and, although she knew it was extremely unlikely, she still harboured hopes of finding Joanna.

'Let's take a picnic on Sunday and even if the place is completely unsuitable for our business, we can turn the day into an outing.'

Neither of them had anticipated Laindon to be such a bustling town. It was not as well established as Guildford, nor as wealthy, but there was an air of optimism and potential. Even though the shops were shut, Madeleine and Flora could see this was a thriving community — even better, they found a double-fronted shop at one end of the High Road which was for sale.

'I'll telephone the estate agent tomorrow,' Flora said, writing the agent's contact details in her notebook. 'We'll arrange to come and view the the shop and rooms . . . that is, if you want to,' she added, noticing Madeleine's reticence.

The reason for looking in Laindon had been because of the possibility of finding Joanna. Madeleine knew the chances were slim of locating her half-sister but even if Joanna wasn't here, it was as good a place as any. Hugh Mansfield hadn't returned to Maison Dubois since they'd reported him to the police, but she had seen him in the distance and she was sure he was following her. They already had someone interested in buying their shop and if they were to move to Laindon, she wouldn't have to keep looking over her shoulder.

'Yes, I want to,' Madeleine said firmly.

* * *

There had been no Closing Down sign at Maison Dubois, and until shortly before they moved to Laindon, only their trusted clients knew they were going. Madeleine had implied that she and Flora would be joining Isabelle in

France because her grandmother had been sick, which explained the speed of their departure. Many of their customers knew about Hugh Mansfield's obsession with Isabelle and had heard about his night-time visit. Several had seen the bruises on Madeleine's face and wrist and had assured her they wouldn't allow him to find out that she'd gone to be with her family.

Madeleine and Flora had been sad at deceiving so many loyal customers.

'When we get established, we could let some of the ladies who live in London know where we've set up. It's not a very long trip on the train to Laindon,' Flora said.

But they both knew that before that happened, their customers would find alternative places to buy their fashions and forget Maison Dubois.

As soon as Isabelle came home, Madeleine was going to suggest they change the name of the business to Maison Maréchal. It would be a fresh start all round and make it harder for Hugh to trace them.

13

While the sale was going through on the shop and flat in Guildford, Isabelle and Hélène stayed in a hotel in London rather than risk drawing Hugh Mansfield back into their lives.

Madeleine's fears that they might not like the new shop in Essex were unfounded and as soon as the purchase was complete, they threw themselves into the move, cleaning and organising the shop and work areas.

It had taken a while to build a new client base although most of the customers required plain garments and simple hats — nothing like they'd produced in Guildford. When they weren't working on orders, Isabelle, Flora and Madeleine made more elaborate garments to show in the windows.

'Nothing as fancy as we had in Maison Dubois,' Flora said. 'But something eye-catching that'll hopefully draw people into the shop.

One morning, a letter arrived from Mrs Richardson on expensive stationery, requesting the presence of the proprietor of Maison Maréchal at Priory Hall at eleven o'clock the following day. It was suggested that samples of fabric be brought. A few enquiries revealed that Priory Hall was a large house about a mile from Laindon High Road which belonged to Mr Ranulph Richardson, of Richardson, Bailey and Cole, solicitors, whose premises were almost opposite Maison Maréchal.

'The aristocracy of Laindon,' Ronnie Bennett, their next-door neighbour told them. 'I don't hold with it meself,' he added, 'I thought after the war, things'd be different. None of this landed gentry nonsense. But if his wife has asked for you,' he nodded in the direction of the offices of Richardson, Bailey and Cole, 'you might find you do very nicely out of it. The family are loaded.'

'This could be the opportunity we've been looking for,' said Flora excitedly. 'We need to plan this trip with military precision. Why don't you take Madeleine along? It'll be good experience.'

Isabelle agreed and Madeleine threw Flora a grateful look. It would be exciting to visit Priory Hall, but mostly she'd be there to keep an eye on her mother. When Isabelle and Hélène had arrived, Flora and Madeleine had noticed how quiet they were. The enthusiasm Isabelle had shown for the business before she'd left for France had disappeared. Instead, an air of sad wistfulness hung over her, and Hélène was often seen observing her daughter with mournful eyes. If her lack of commitment should become obvious to Mrs Richardson, Madeleine would inject a bit of enthusiasm. There had been a great deal of expense with repairs to Château Bellevais and the removal of their belongings to Essex. Maison Maréchal was doing well — but nowhere near as well as it needed if they were to remain solvent.

'She'll tell us what's worrying her when she's ready, Maddie,' Flora said. 'Perhaps she's worried Hélène won't settle down here. She's had a lot of upheaval and leaving your home can be difficult. And of course, we need to find more clients. Let's give them both time.'

⋆ ⋆ ⋆

Ronnie and his sister, Maud, owned the hardware store next door to Maison Maréchal and had been very helpful when Isabelle and the others first arrived.

'I could give you a lift in the van tomorrow. I'll put a clean cloth over the seat. Can't have you ladies going to Priory Hall with dirty skirts!' He guffawed with laughter. 'Mrs Richardson's a bit of a snob by all accounts.

The likes o' her don't come into hardware shops. But don't take no nonsense from her, that's my advice.'

The following day, he drove them through the narrow lanes to Priory Hall.

'I'll be waiting right here to take you home, so don't you worry about a thing.'

'I'm not sure Mrs Richardson will be happy about a van parked in front of the house, if she's as much a snob as Ronnie claims,' whispered Isabelle as they waited at the front door. 'D'you think we should have gone round the back?'

Before Madeleine could reply, a maid answered the door and showed them into Mrs Richardson's drawing room.

*   *   *

The order for a green velvet gown had gone extremely successfully and was followed by instructions for an outfit for a garden party. The matching dress,

209

jacket and hat had been so admired by the other guests that Maison Maréchal became popular almost overnight.

For Isabelle and Madeleine, the financial pressure was relieved and there was even enough income to afford to employ a young girl to help in the shop. The popularity of Maison Maréchal meant that Mrs Richardson no longer demanded that either Isabelle or Madeleine go to Priory Hall with samples. Knowing the shop was busy, she was so determined her order be fulfilled before any of the other customer's that if it meant the chauffeur had to bring her to town to visit the shop herself, then so be it.

One morning while Madeleine was shaping feathers with a curling iron in the kitchen, Molly, their young shop girl, rushed in.

'Please, ma'am, Mrs Richardson's here to pick up an order. Miss Flora's stepped out to buy a newspaper and Mrs Maréchal's taken her mother out for a walk. Would you like me to serve her?'

Madeleine rose, knowing that Mrs Richardson wouldn't be happy being served by a young girl. She barely had any time for Madeleine but at least acknowledged she was the proprietor's daughter.

When she entered the shop, Mrs Richardson wasn't there. Madeleine shot a look of annoyance at Molly, who didn't notice because she was looking expectantly at the young woman who was peering at the brooches.

'Mrs Richardson,' said Molly, bobbing a curtsey and throwing out her hand, to indicate the young woman.

'Good morning,' said the young woman turning and holding out her hand 'You must be Miss Maréchal.' Catching the surprise on Madeleine's face, she added 'I'm Mrs Richardson, and I've come to pick up my mother-in-law's hat.'

'M . . . Mrs Richardson?' For the second time in her life, Madeleine had the feeling she was looking into a mirror that was reflecting a slightly older image of herself.

'Yes, I'm Mrs Ben Richardson. My mother-in-law, Mrs Ranulph Richardson, asked me to pick up . . . are you all right? You've gone very white.'

'Yes, I'm fine, thank you,' Madeleine said, feeling foolish. 'I stood up too quickly,' she lied.

'Oh, I know what that's like. When I was expecting my daughter, Faye, I often came over dizzy. Are you all right now?'

'Oh, yes, thank you. I'll fetch the hat.'

Madeleine rushed out of the shop into the store room and stood with her back to the door, waiting for her heartbeat to steady. It was impossible to be certain because she'd only seen Joanna once, but it seemed that her half-sister was on the other side of the door!

Madeleine took the hat out of the candy-striped hat box and showed the young woman.

'It's absolutely beautiful,' she said wistfully, 'My mother-in-law will look wonderful.'

'I'm sure you'll look lovely too.'

The woman was silent for a moment as if trying to make up her mind whether to trust Madeleine. Finally she said, 'I probably won't be going. I've been invited, of course, but — '

The strident whistling of the kettle cut through the air stopping the conversation. After a brief pause to see if Molly would turn the stove off, Madeleine shook her head in annoyance.

'As you can hear, the water's boiled. I was about to make tea when you arrived. Perhaps you've time to join me, Mrs Richardson?'

'Yes, thank you, I'd love that. And please call me Joanna.'

* * *

Joanna took her daughter Faye to Priory Hall several times a week to

213

spend time with her grandmother, and after dropping her off she carried on into town and stopped at Maison Maréchal. Madeleine longed to tell Joanna they were sisters, knowing that she was being deceitful in keeping it from her, but whenever Joanna spoke about her father — *their* father — her tone became soft and it was evident that she'd loved him very much.

Madeleine knew she could never betray his secret. How would Joanna feel if she knew what had happened in France all those years ago? Instead, she encouraged Joanna to talk about both parents, just so she could hear stories about her father. From time to time, Joanna brought her daughter, Faye, into the shop and Madeleine was thrilled to know she had a niece as well as a sister.

When Joanna confided she wasn't going to her mother-in-law's garden party because she couldn't afford to buy a dress, Madeleine was amazed. 'But I thought your family was rich.'

'My parents-in-law are very well off, but when Ben announced he was marrying me, his mother told him she wouldn't give him a penny. He's never asked for anything since. We're comfortable — we have our own house, nothing like Priory Hall, of course — and Ben earns a good salary but we like to be independent. Of course, now we have Faye, Mother-in-law loves to spoil her, buying her whatever she likes. But Ben is proud and even if we needed anything, he'd rather do without than ask his mother. Ben will go to the garden party and stay a while but I don't want to go and show him up by wearing something shabby when everyone else will be so well-dressed.'

Madeleine knew that Faye would look beautiful in a lovely pink dress Flora had made — paid for by Joanna's mother-in-law. It was so unfair that Joanna was not accepted by her husband's family. It was all very well being loved by the sister she didn't know she had and who longed to make herself known, but it was no consolation.

'Would you go if you had a suitable dress?' Madeleine asked.

'Well, I'd love to go and make Ben proud of me but I don't know many of my mother-in-law's friends and those I do know don't approve of me.'

'I've had an idea. One of our customers wanted a dress made and we ordered the beautiful pale blue fabric she chose, but when she came in for a fitting she said the colour didn't suit her. Would you believe she decided she wanted a different design in red!' Madeleine hoped her little lie sounded more convincing to Joanna's ears than it did to hers. 'She was about the same size as you and I'm sure with a little adjustment, it would be perfect for you. Of course, it would be a fraction of the cost our client would have paid.'

'Really?' Joanna said, her face alive with hope.

'You'd be doing us a favour. Let me take your measurements; when you next come in, I'll have it altered to fit. We can always lend you a hat.'

★　★　★

'That's very extravagant,' Flora remarked when Madeleine told her what she was going to do. 'But very kind. It's lovely that you two young women have become such good friends.'

Madeleine wondered whether she should tell Flora they were actually more than friends but decided against it. She trusted Flora, of course, but it seemed better to keep it to herself — the fewer people who knew, the less likely the secret would be discovered. But it wouldn't have been possible to hide her dress-making plans from Flora. Isabelle still seemed very distracted and hadn't noticed what her daughter was doing.

Madeleine worked late into the night, firstly to get the day's jobs finished and then to start on Joanna's dress. The design she had in mind would be simple but elegant with black Chantilly lace on the bodice, and she had a hat that would be a wonderful match. She would pretend it was hers and offer it to Joanna to borrow.

The dress fit perfectly and Joanna was thrilled with it. 'I can't thank you enough. It's beautiful!'

'It's a pleasure,' said Madeleine. Her eyes ached and her shoulders and neck were knotted from the late nights she'd spent making sure the dress was ready.

'So, will you come?' Joanna asked.

Madeleine stifled a yawn, 'Sorry?'

'To the garden party at Priory Hall.'

'Me?'

'Yes, Mother-in-law was in a really good mood earlier when I dropped Faye off and she asked me if I wanted to bring a friend.'

'I'd love to, but are you sure she won't mind?'

'She told me I could bring a friend, and I'd like to take you.'

The fund-raising garden party had been one of the social highlights of the year and Madeleine had enjoyed it very much despite the rather awkward incident on their arrival.

When Mrs Richardson saw who her daughter-in-law had invited, her expression hardened and her eyes closed to narrow slits. Madeleine and Joanna stood like startled rabbits as she walked purposely towards them, but before she could reach them she was intercepted by Lady Rothersmere.

'Mrs Richardson, may I say this is a beautiful occasion. Lord Rothersmere and I are so pleased to be here. And just look at the weather. Absolutely perfect. You seem to have thought of everything — even the blue skies!'

Mrs Richardson allowed herself to be distracted from the presence of a common seamstress at her party. 'Oh, thank you Lady Rothersmere. That's very kind of you to say such things about our little gathering.'

'Little gathering? Nonsense! This is a marvellous occasion. It's very generous of you to be raising money for so many good causes, and may I say, so avant-garde!'

'Avant-garde?'

'Yes, indeed! I hear the designer of your delightful outfit is here. I love artists, don't you? I hear she has links with the wonderful Jean-Luc Maurier. Would you mind introducing me to your designer? I promise not to steal her, but I'm planning a masqued ball — to which you and Mr Richardson are invited, of course — and I need someone young with imagination and flair.'

A large sum of money for charity was raised that day, but they weren't the only ones to benefit. Mrs Richardson's reputation as a woman of fashion and style was enhanced by having patronised such a talented young designer. Aware of the close friendship between Mademoiselle Maréchal and her daughter-in-law, she became more tolerant of Joanna — at least in public — which pleased Joanna and Ben.

Maison Maréchal's clientele rapidly multiplied, resulting in Molly being employed full-time and three new seamstresses being engaged.

And Madeleine? She was enjoying getting to know her family — albeit in secret and from afar.

14

James worked at the office into the night, often falling asleep at his desk in an effort to complete the project quickly.

'This is going to have to stop, James,' Michel said when he realised how much time he was spending at work. 'You're going to start making mistakes and that will put us behind.'

James had gone home early that night but was in before anyone else the next morning and already working before the cleaner arrived. He paused to raise his feet while she mopped under his chair and he suddenly remembered Madame Picard doing so in the kitchen at the château.

The longing for Isabelle seized him again and just as he was about turn back to his work, it occurred to him that he hadn't received a response to his telegram. He'd explained that he wouldn't be able to go with them on the journey to England as he'd hoped, but that he'd follow on as soon as he'd finished his job. And he'd asked her for the address in Guildford.

Perhaps she'd been too busy packing up to reply. After all, it was an enormous undertaking to move to England and to decide what to take and what to leave behind.

At lunchtime, he went out and sent another telegram to Montplessis, then returned and, against Michel's advice, stayed until midnight.

The day of Isabelle and Hélène's departure, came and went, and still there was no word from her. Surely something would arrive soon? In desperation, he telephoned the Post Office at Montplessis and asked the post mistress if she knew if Madame Rousseau and her daughter had already left Château Bellevais and if it would be possible to get a message to them. The post mistress curtly told him she had no idea about Madame Rousseau's whereabouts and appeared to be about to hang up.

'Please!' he shouted down the receiver. 'If you see them, let them know I haven't received their address in England.'

He wasn't sure whether she'd heard him or if she'd cut the call before he'd finished.

★　★　★

As soon as Michel and the clients were happy with the plans and drawings, James packed all his belongings. He hadn't amassed much during the years he'd been in Caen and anything that didn't fit into his two suitcases was given away.

His journey to Guildford had been relatively problem-free — the worst part would be finding Maison Dubois. The receptionist in the hotel he'd booked into knew Maison Dubois well and insisted on going into the office to bring out the hat she'd bought there. James was impatient for her to tell him where the shop was, but instead, he politely admired it and asked again for the address, which she scribbled on a piece of paper.

'There's no point going now, they'll be closed,' she called after him but he'd already gone.

The girl had given him the correct address. It said Maison Dubois on the sign over the door — but the shop was empty. The street was deserted and all the surrounding shops were shut for the day. There was nothing for it, he'd have to wait until morning and see if he could find out from Isabelle's neighbours where she'd gone.

He walked dejectedly back to the hotel, the bouquet he'd bought for Isabelle hanging downwards, the flowers scraping the pavement.

★ ★ ★

At the mention of Isabelle's name, people's faces changed from open and friendly to guarded and suspicious. Several of her neighbours had asked his name and enquired whether he was a friend of Hugh Mansfield.

'Who is he?' he'd asked but no one was prepared to say, other than the newsagent next to where Maison Dubois had once been.

'A nutcase, that's who,' he said. 'Frightening that poor young girl like that.'

'Please, I'm a friend of Madame Maréchal,' James said, trying his best to sound rational and reasonable. 'It's really important that I find her.' He handed the man his business card which he hoped might impress him into giving more information.

'An architect, eh?'

James nodded. 'I'd really appreciate it if you could tell me anything.'

Several small boys entered the shop, jostling each other and drawing the newsagent's attention away from James.

He looked James up and down and decided that he could be trusted,

'The ladies have moved to Essex. Laindon, I think. That's all I know. Now if you'll excuse me . . . '

He marched over to the boys and grabbed one of them by the ear.

'I'll 'ave none of yer thieving nonsense, laddie,' he said and led the boy outside. The others followed, leaving James alone in the shop.

Essex. That was a large county. But the man had also said London. Did he mean that they'd moved to the East End of London which bordered on Essex? That made sense because he knew there were lots of tailors and dress shops in the East End.

If the newsagent knew that much, surely one of Isabelle's neighbours could give him more details? But if they could, no one would. Several people said they hadn't seen her since she'd gone to France months ago and others expressed disbelief that the shop was closed.

Eventually, one nervous shopkeeper threatened to telephone the police if he didn't stop asking questions.

James went back to the hotel and asked at reception if he could look in the telephone directory but there was no entry for Maison Dubois.

'Perhaps they haven't had a telephone installed yet?' the girl who'd shown him her hat suggested. 'What a shame they've gone. They had the nicest clothes in Guildford. I'll ask a few of my friends to see if they know where it's gone.'

Eventually, James had to admit he'd lost Isabelle.

15

Hélène was sitting at the table with Isabelle, Flora and Madeleine, listening to the BBC broadcast on the radio set. Great Britain and France had just declared war on Germany.

'Not again! Surely not again!' she wailed. 'I really thought it could be sorted out diplomatically.'

Madeleine looked at each of the shocked faces and knew they were reliving moments from the Great War — the war that was supposed to have ended all wars. Mémé's husband, Pépé Philippe, and Flora's fiancé, Peter, had both died during the fighting, and both women would undoubtedly be thinking about how different their lives would have been had their men lived. And of course, Maman would be remembering Tom Marshall.

'What will it mean for us?' Madeleine asked but no one replied. Haunted eyes looked through her as if peering into a dreadful abyss. Strangely, it was Maman who seemed most upset. Tears had begun to flow down her cheeks and Hélène placed a comforting hand over her daughter's.

'I have to go back,' she whispered. 'I have to at least hear it from his own mouth.'

'Yes, Chérie. I understand but I think it's time to tell Madeleine and Flora,' said Hélène.

Isabelle nodded. 'Yes, it's time.'

★   ★   ★

'I knew there was something wrong,' said Flora. 'You came back from France a different woman. But why didn't you contact him?'

'He said he'd send word but he didn't. It all happened so fast and he obviously had second thoughts. I didn't want to put pressure on him. If he'd decided not to come, it was best he didn't.'

'Perhaps he had an accident. You can't be sure he changed his mind,' said Madeleine.

'He'd have got word to me somehow.'

'If he was so right for you, I find it hard to believe he'd let you down like that. Why didn't you just telephone him?'

'I couldn't. We didn't exchange addresses. There was no need for me to know where he lived as he was going to come to England. I don't even know the name of the company he worked for — just that it's in Caen, in Normandy, and the director is Michel, but I don't know his surname.'

'Then why are you going back, Maman?' Madeleine asked.

'Because I remember what it was like during the last war and how fragile life is. I realise I can't bear not to see him once more. And if he tells me to my face that he doesn't want me, then I'll come home and live with it. But if there's a chance . . . '

'But how will you find him, Maman?'

'I'll go to Caen and search.'

'Don't be angry, Chérie,' said Hélène. 'But I asked Henriette Girardot in the Post Office to find all the architectural companies in Caen, especially those whose directors have the initial M. She told me she couldn't find any. If I'd discovered one, I'd have telephoned them myself. It's going to be like looking for a needle in a haystack.'

'I'll come with you and help you look, Maman.'

'No, Chérie, thank you, but no. I don't suppose the Germans will invade France like they did last time but it still might be dangerous and I need to know the three of you are safe here, looking after our business. I'll go and check the château too. There are several valuable paintings and legal documents we left behind. I might as well bring back anything I can carry. It may be a while before we can go back to France.'

'It's nearly Christmas, Maman, please don't leave until the new year,' Madeleine begged, secretly hoping her mother would change her mind about chasing after a man who had not even bothered to let her know he had decided against moving to England to be with her.

★   ★   ★

Early in the new year, Hélène caught influenza and after her earlier bout of pneumonia, it was several weeks before she was better. Just as she recovered, first Flora, then Madeleine succumbed, and finally Isabelle became ill too.

Severe winter storms delayed Isabelle even more and it wasn't until April, 1940 that she set foot once more on French soil . . .

Isabelle booked into the Hotel Lion d'Or in Caen. Didier Lajoie, the proprietor — a talkative man who wanted to try his English out on her once he discovered she'd been living in England — knew of two architectural companies. He thought there would probably be others too, either in the city or the surrounding towns, and called his wife from the kitchen to see if she knew of any. He gave her a list of three companies and their addresses at dinner that evening.

'Are you having something built?' he asked.

'Didier, leave the poor woman alone! It's none of your business,' Madame Lajoie said. 'I'm so sorry, Madame, my husband is incorrigible!' she said as she ladled soup into Isabelle's bowl.

Isabelle laughed. 'I'm just looking for a friend,' she said. 'We didn't get a chance to say goodbye.'

* * *

She rose early and made her way through rainy streets to the nearest company on Didier's list.

The receptionist in Joubert Vannier

234

Architects said that they didn't have an architect by the name of James Hart, although it sounded rather familiar and she was sure she'd heard of him.

'I've definitely heard the name before . . . ' She thought for a moment. 'I have a feeling he might work at Atelier Architecture Michel Passereau on the other side of the city — but I might be wrong. I can telephone them to make sure, if you like?'

'Yes please, that would be very kind.'

The receptionist placed the receiver back in the cradle. 'Well, I was right, he did work there but apparently he's left.'

'Left?' Isabelle's stomach lurched. She hadn't expected it would be easy to track James down, but to find his company only to immediately lose him again was a great blow.

Isabelle decided to go to Atelier Architecture Michel Passereau to see if anyone knew where James had gone, hoping he might still be in Caen. She was drenched by the time she got there. The receptionist told her that Michel

Passereau was out on site somewhere and probably wouldn't be back for several hours, but Isabelle decided to wait. She had nothing better to do and she needed to find out what had happened to James.

The receptionist had started two weeks before and didn't know where James had gone — she hadn't even met him, so Isabelle knew he'd been gone a fortnight. He could be anywhere by now.

When he returned, Michel showed Isabelle into his office.

'So you're the lady who lured my best architect away. I have to tell you, Madame, you've done me a great disservice. James was an excellent architect and a good friend. What I don't understand is, why you're here looking for him. Surely he went to England to be with you?'

'No, I didn't hear from him, so my mother and I went back to England on our own. I thought he'd changed his mind and decided to stayed here.'

'No, he handed in his notice although he worked on the project I'd taken on earlier. When it was finished, he left. He said you hadn't replied to his telegrams, so he was going to Montplessis.'

'Telegrams? I didn't receive any telegrams!' Isabelle felt the blood draining from her face. 'Do you know where he is now?'

'No, I'm sorry, I've no idea. He's probably in England now, waiting at your home.'

'He didn't have the address and even if he had, we moved to another town. He'll never find us.' Isabelle could feel panic rising in her throat. So, he *had* wanted to be with her but somehow they'd missed each other!

Michel ordered coffee for her and insisted she leave her new address in case he should hear from James, but a client arrived for a meeting and he offered his apologies and left her in the office with the receptionist.

It was dark before she got back to the hotel and she bathed and changed into dry clothes. Tomorrow, she would check out of the hotel and go to Montplessis. The only place they had in common was the château. Perhaps Madame Picard or Étienne had seen him. Perhaps he'd left an address where she could contact him.

16

The terrible news of the evacuation at Dunkirk at the end of May 1940 brought home the seriousness of the situation to James.

He'd found himself a room in London and a job in an architect's office. Michel had asked him to open an office in London but his heart hadn't been in it. Instead, in his spare time, he roamed around the East End of London, wondering if this was a place where a fashionable shop would have opened. Many of the Victorian slums had been demolished but still there was evidence of poverty and overcrowded housing. Many cobbled streets were lined with grimy, terraced houses from which scruffy children spilled, while women in aprons and scarves tied over their curlers, scrubbed at doorsteps or set off to the shops with baskets over their arms and several children sitting on, or hanging from, battered prams.

The more he wandered, the more certain he was that Isabelle's shop was not there and he extended his search further into Essex.

However, on September the seventh, 1940, James knew that his life of self-indulgent searching would have to take second place to more important events.

Hitler's promise of retaliation following a bombing raid on Berlin proved to be the start of months of heavy and frequent bombing attacks, many of which took place at night and targeted areas such as docks and factories.

James joined the Rescue Services of the Air Raid Precautions. He'd tried to join up but had failed his medical exam because of shrapnel wounds he'd sustained during the Great War, and when the doctor had seen his disappointment, he'd commented that since James had experience of living and working in France for so long, he might be more useful to the country helping in some way other than fighting.

'Would you like me to pull a few strings?' he asked, and James had said that he would.

* * *

By late 1941, James was back in France, this time working for the secret Special Operations Executive whose purpose was to spy, carry out reconnaissance and sabotage, and assist any French resistance.

With his artistic skills, he'd proved to be a gifted forger of the identity papers French citizens needed to present to the authorities. Providing false papers to members of the Resistance allowed them to live double lives without detection.

He'd requested his senior officer at SOE that he remain in the Picardie region, arguing that he'd served there during the Great War and had spent time in that area since. He didn't draw attention to the fact that he was probably more familiar with Caen, wanting to serve anywhere near Montplessis. However tenuous, it was the only link he still had with Isabelle.

★   ★   ★

The twin-engine Whitley banked as the pilot searched for the signal lights below and James held on tightly. He looked at his fellow operative, David Solomon, who was also ready to jump out into the night sky.

James wouldn't be sorry to leave the aeroplane. The fuselage reeked of oil and they had encountered pockets of turbulence as they flew low to avoid enemy detection. It had been an uncomfortable ride. James and David were both pale and nervous — as newly trained operatives, they would be dropped into occupied France and have to live on their wits.

The briefing officer had done a

last-minute check on their cover story before they departed. James's code name was Arlequin, which he would use when communicating with SOE, and his field name was Luc Moret. David would be known as Robert Lameau.

Both of them had been supplied with tablets to keep them awake and a suicide pill if the unthinkable happened and they were captured by the Gestapo. They carried maps, French Francs, a compass, small fighting knives, chocolate, and four canisters would be dropped with them, containing guns, explosives and forgery materials.

Finally, the pilot located the landing lights and James and David jumped into the cold night air, hanging briefly as their parachutes opened and then landed in a field. James was dragged some way before he came to a stop and stripped off the parachute harness and flying suit, beneath which he wore dark trousers and jacket.

He checked for David who'd jumped

before him and saw him gathering up his parachute on the far side of the field. From behind the hedge, two men ran towards James with guns raised.

'Code?' one of them said.

'The clown is on the merry-go-round.'

'Name?'

'Luc Moret.'

'And your friend?'

'He is Robert Lameau,' James replied.

The men lowered their guns.

'Thank God you are here. I am Claude Boutet and this is Antoine Valluy. Quickly, let's get rid of your parachutes.'

James and David followed the two Frenchmen to their van and climbed inside among piles of empty vegetable crates.

The lurching and jolting of the van told James that they had left the road and were driving down a heavily rutted path. The van pulled up and the doors were opened, allowing fresh air in to relieve him of the smell of rotting cabbage.

'This is St-Pierre-sur-Somme. Luc will get out here. Robert will stay in another safe house,' Claude said, leading James to the front door of a ramshackle farmhouse.

A tall, thin woman wearing a nightgown opened the door and quickly pulled James inside. Within seconds, the van had turned in the yard and was heading back down the rutted path, taking David to another safe house.

Mathilde Deloffre led James to the huge kitchen, made coffee and poured them each a cognac. She explained she had lost her husband in the Great War and her son had recently died in a labour camp in Germany.

'I have nothing but my life left to lose and when that goes, it will be a blessing. I will join my family. Until then, I will fight with every fibre of my being to get rid of the Boches from my land! Vive la France!' she said, standing and saluting with her cognac glass.

She was indeed a formidable lady and during the following days, James was touched at how much care she took of him. There was always a hot meal ready for him, despite severe food shortages, when he returned from training members of the growing band of Resistance Fighters in firearm and explosives use, as well as the acts of sabotage they carried out on railways, German storage and communication facilities.

'So,' Mathilde said after James had been with her a week. 'Tell me about your life in England. You have a wife? Someone who is missing you?'

James shook his head, 'No, no one.'

'I guessed as much. You have the air of someone who has nothing to lose,' she said, pointing to her chest. 'Just like me. But you are a good-looking man. I don't understand why you are alone.'

James wasn't used to such bluntness but she seemed genuinely concerned rather than nosy, and she obviously felt solidarity with him. Little by little, he told her about meeting Isabelle and staying at Château Bellevais — and how he'd lost touch with her.

'I know of it,' she said, 'I don't believe I've ever seen it but I have a cousin who lives in a village not far from Montplessis. But surely it must be possible to find her. Did you return to the château? Perhaps she left something there for you?'

'I sent her three telegrams and two letters with my address in Caen. If she'd wanted me to join her, she'd have contacted me. The only explanation I could think of is that she had second thoughts because of her daughter. I understand that a child must come first . . . '

'You are expecting a drop of radio equipment tomorrow, n'est ce pas?'

'Yes, I am. The plane will arrive just after midnight. Why?'

'Because you will be free during the day and you and I are going to pay a little visit to my cousin near Montplessis . . . '

Early the following morning Mathilde fired up the wood gas generator on her farm truck and set off with James for Montplessis.

As they approached the entrance to Château Bellevais, a German car turned into the drive and Mathilde slowed down but didn't follow it.

'The Germans have requisitioned it,' she said.

As they drew level with the entrance, they saw several German vehicles outside the château and Mathilde carried on towards the village.

'I'm going to stop and find out,' she said. 'I'll find a quiet place to park. You wait in the van and I'll go for a drink in the bar.'

She reappeared an hour later, smelling of cigarette smoke and cognac, but with a satisfied look on her face.

The owner of the La Pomme Dorée had been surly to the point of rudeness in the beginning, but her childhood memories of exploring the area when she visited her cousin obviously rekindled thoughts of his youth and gradually, they discovered they had mutual acquaintances, Mathilde's cousin being one of them. Luckily, the bar wasn't busy and he had time to talk. Once he overcame his initial reticence, he had opinions on everything and everyone in the village.

The name of one person in particular had come up over and over — Norbert Charbonel. The bartender named other people supposedly either willingly associating with him or under duress because they owed him money.

'Étienne Picard?' asked James.

'Yes, that was one name. How do you know?'

James explained that Madame Picard had told Isabelle that her brother-in-law was in debt to Charbonel after he'd claimed he couldn't get the roofing materials he'd ordered. He'd made an insultingly low offer to buy the château, as it was in such a poor state of repair and unlikely to ever be restored to its former glory and he would take it off Hélène's hands.

'Apparently he was the person who drew the German's attention to the château and suggested they might like to commandeer it,' Mathilde said.

James sighed and thought of the love that Hélène and Isabelle had for the place. If the Germans won the war, they would be unlikely to reimburse Hélène. And if the Allies won, what sort of state would it be in when the Germans left?

'There are other people Charbonel seems to have control over,' Mathilde said. 'Like the woman in the Post Office. Her son is seriously ill and Charbonel gives her money for treatment. In exchange he demands she keeps her ears open for information which she gives to Charbonel. The bartender said she tampers with letters and telegrams. And then there's the policeman. He was caught with another woman and Charbonel is blackmailing him, too. There are others. It might be worth giving this information to the Resistance. They can pass on it on to Resistance fighters in the area. A collaborator is a danger to France and its people.'

'Tampers with letters and telegrams?' whispered James. 'Is it possible?'

'Ah,' said Mathilde, realising his train of thought. 'You think she might not have delivered your telegrams to Isabelle?'

'Possibly, but I don't see how it would affect Charbonel. Once Isabelle and her mother were in England, it wouldn't matter if I went or not.'

'There's only one way to be sure,' said Mathilde. 'We'll find the woman and see what she gives away.'

'We can't do that. We might jeopardise the operation here — she'd be bound to tell Charbonel. I want to know the truth but I can't risk so many people's lives just to satisfy my curiosity. Suppose she didn't have anything to do with Isabelle not replying to my telegrams and letters? I'd have given us away for nothing.'

'We'll tell the Resistance and see what they think. If Monsieur Norbert Charbonel can be removed, all sorts of tongues may wag, and who knows what they might tell us?'

★　★　★

James didn't know if Monsieur Charbonel met with a genuine accident or not. It seemed a coincidence that shortly after Mathilde had brought Claude's attention to the suspected collaborator, his body was found in a burned-out car not far from Château Bellevais. It was discovered upside down in a ditch and no other vehicle appeared to have been involved.

Mathilde found out from the bartender of La Pomme Dorée when the funeral would be held and was one of the few who attended. Mostly, the villagers avoided the service, Monsieur Charbonel being well known as a bully.

On her way from the church, she stopped at the Post Office to send a telegram: *Cousin Norbert buried today. Stop. Very sad. Stop. Mathilde.*

As she dictated, she watched the young woman's face; her top lip was curled with distaste.

'Did you know my cousin Norbert?' Mathilde asked innocently.

'Yes.' There was no mistaking the contempt.

'I noticed there weren't many mourners at the funeral. Was he not well liked in Montplessis?'

'Not really,' said the woman. 'Although I'm sorry for your loss,' she added. Obviously feeling she needed to explain herself, she said, 'He had a way of making people do what he wanted.'

'Oh? How d'you mean?'

'Well, I wouldn't want to say anything against someone who's not even cold in their grave, and your cousin as well . . . '

'Distant cousin,' said Mathilde. 'And

253

truth be told, I didn't really like him much. He always bullied me as a child,' she lied.

'Ah,' said the post mistress. 'You've hit the nail on the head. He was a bully.'

'Forgive me, Madame, but you speak with such feeling that I wonder if you have some reason to dislike him.'

The woman looked over Mathilde's shoulders to make sure no one was about to enter the Post Office. 'I'm about to take a break. Would you like a cup of coffee? I only have barley coffee but it might warm you after standing at a graveside.'

'How kind,' said Mathilde, following her into the back room.

★　★　★

'Apparently Charbonel was paying for Henriette's son's medicine. In return, he told her to hand over any telegrams or letters you sent.'

'But why?' asked James.

'Apparently, he wanted to keep you away from Isabelle because the more the château fell into disrepair, the cheaper it would eventually be when Isabelle's mother was forced to sell. He knew you were an architect and feared that you and Isabelle would renovate the château and he'd never get his hands on it. There also seemed to be some spite aimed at Isabelle for rejecting his marriage proposal some years ago,' Mathilde said.

James clenched and unclenched his fists. 'His vindictiveness and greed have lost me Isabelle!'

'Not necessarily, Luc.' Mathilde put her bony hand on his shoulder. 'Isabelle telephoned her and left her new address in case you should go there. Henriette wrote the address down but didn't tell Charbonel.'

'Do you have it?' James stood, his eyes wide with hope. Mathilde handed him a slip of paper. 'Laindon!' He stared at the paper and groaned. 'I thought the newsagent said London! I wasted all that time searching . . . ' He shook his head. 'Now I know where she is, but how can I get a message to her? I can't just post a letter to England!'

'You leave that to me. I can get a letter smuggled out to the Unoccupied Zone or Spain and then it will go by ordinary post to England. At least Isabelle will know where you are. All you have to do is stay alive.'

Letters sent from the Unoccupied Zone were subject to scrutiny and censorship although many postal workers allowed material that the Germans and French Authorities would not have approved of to pass.

While James was out that night helping Claude and Antoine set explosives near a German storage depot, Mathilde wrote a letter. It would be better if it went via Spain but she would have to rely on a courier, so just in case it had to go through the Unoccupied Zone, she wrote in her most flowery handwriting and signed it *Mathilde*. A letter from a woman might draw less

256

attention than one from a man . . .

My dearest Isabelle,

Just a short letter to tell you that our friend, James is well and safe.

She paused. What else could she write without giving vital information away? She couldn't give her address, so there was no chance that Isabelle would be able to reply. She wasn't even sure that it was wise to write James's name, but everyone knew him as Luc Moret, so it was unlikely to be traced back to him. If only there was a way of giving Isabelle a clue about James's location without risk of discovery by the Germans.

The following day when he returned — if he returned, for this raid they had planned was more audacious than any they had carried out before — she would ask him if there was anything she could add that only Isabelle understood, which would give her a hint of James's whereabouts.

James didn't arrive back until just before morning light. A German sentry had almost stumbled across Claude when he was setting the last of the explosives and he had to take a circuitous route back to where the others were hidden in the undergrowth. The explosion had blown most of the depot away but it had alerted a patrol which by chance had not been far away and James, Claude and Antoine had less time than they'd anticipated to escape.

Searchlights played over the fields while soldiers with rifles at the ready combed the ground where the Resistance fighters were hiding. James, Claude and Antoine managed to reach the woods and then separated, increasing the chance that at least one of them would return.

Mathilde had waited for James, pacing the kitchen and keeping the kettle boiling, ready to make him barley coffee when he returned.

Yes, when *he returns*, she told herself.

She'd heard an explosion from the

direction of the German storage depot and hoped the mission had been successful. It should have taken James an hour to arrive back at the farmhouse but three hours later, he hadn't returned.

When he finally did appear, he was limping and covered in leaves, twigs and mud where he'd snaked on his stomach through the undergrowth. His face and hands were cut and his trousers were torn, but at least he was alive.

She cleaned his cuts and tidied everything away. If a German patrol should come by, there would be no evidence that anyone had disturbed her night. James was hidden in the loft, the door to which was concealed behind a large cupboard that had to be moved each time he came and went. It was difficult for her to move on her own but at least it wouldn't attract attention. This time, as she placed her shoulder to the heavy, wooden cupboard to move it back into position, there was a pounding on her door. It lent her strength as she shoved the cupboard back, then went downstairs to open the door.

It was, as she had suspected, a German patrol. James had told her that the damage he, Claude and Antoine had caused was considerable. Minor acts of sabotage had been ignored by the Germans but this would need investigation and, Mathilde was certain, there would be reprisals.

She opened the door, rubbing her eyes as if she had just got out of bed. 'Monsieur?' she said to the officer on the doorstep.

'Out of my way,' he said rudely, barging past Mathilde and beckoning to his soldiers to follow.

'What is the meaning of this?' Mathilde said, as if shocked at their appearance.

'We are looking for saboteurs. Get out of my way, Madame, do not delay me.'

'But there's no one here but me!'

'Then you have nothing to fear.' He strode through her kitchen towards the stairs.

She'd taken the precaution of making her bed appear as if she had just got out of it but it would, of course, be cold and it would be obvious she had not just left it. All she could do was pray that he was too busy looking for men to worry about the temperature of her bed.

She followed the soldiers upstairs. As expected, they were looking in each room, in cupboards and wardrobes — anywhere that a man might hide.

She suddenly noticed that, in her haste to move the cupboard covering the small door to the attic where James was now hiding, she had rucked up the mat! She walked to it and stood on it, trying to conceal it with her feet. Mathilde's heart was beating so fast, she wondered if the officer could hear it!

Finally, satisfied there was no one in her house, the Germans left.

Her arms and legs suddenly felt so weak, it was a while before she thought she'd be able to shift the cupboard and let James out. It made sense to wait, anyway. It wasn't unknown for Germans to return to a property they'd already searched in the hope that people had been lulled into a false sense of security and anyone hiding would then be caught.

James was almost frantic when Mathilde finally moved the cupboard and let him out. He'd heard the soldiers leave but then there had been silence while Mathilde waited, and he'd feared they'd arrested her.

'Did they hurt you?' he asked.

'No, I'm fine. Let's hope Claude and Antoine had as much luck as you.'

She collected eggs from the hen house and made two large omelettes. While they ate, she showed him the letter she'd written.

'Is there anything I can write to let Isabelle know where you are without giving anything away?'

James thought for a moment.

'No,' he said, 'Nothing you can write ... but there is something we can send.'

He took the writing pad and closed his eyes, remembering her the day he'd kissed her by the lake. With swift, sure strokes, he drew Isabelle sitting by the lake with a Labrador next to her. Would she remember the day the dog and his master had disturbed them?

If she did she would realise that when Mathilde added *P S — J is near this lake*, and she would know roughly where he was.

*   *   *

The letter was given to a courier who carried it across the Pyrenees to Spain where it was posted to England. Several weeks after James had drawn Isabelle sitting by the lake, the letter was in her hands.

Madeleine brought the post to the breakfast table where she, Hélène,

Flora and Isabelle sat.

'There's a bill and a letter from . . . ' she scrutinised the stamp, 'Spain, for you, Maman.'

'Spain?' Isabelle took the letter and inspected the loopy handwriting before slitting the envelope open with a knife.

'Who's it from?' asked Flora, observing Isabelle's puzzled frown.

'Someone called Mathilde telling me our friend, James, is well,' she said staring at the paper.

'What d'you think James is doing in Spain?' Hélène asked. 'And why didn't he write himself?'

Isabelle gasped as she saw her portrait and recognised the location. If there had been any doubt, the Labrador clinched it.

'He's not in Spain, he's in France!' she gasped, her hands flying to her throat.

'But the letter came from Spain, Maman.'

'I know, Chérie, but I'm sure he's in France, not far from Montplessis.

Although who Mathilde is, I have no idea. I don't remember him ever mentioning anyone of that name.'

Her heart lurched. Had he found someone else? Had Mathilde discovered about her and decided to warn her that James was no longer interested in her? But why had she included the portrait which had definitely been drawn by James? Why hadn't *he* written? And if Mathilde and James were in France, wasn't it rather excessive to get a letter out of France to Spain and then to England, just to warn Isabelle off? So many questions and the only thing that brought her any joy was knowing that James was still alive!

'If James is in France, how d'you think the letter got to Spain?' Madeleine asked.

But then Hélène explained about the couriers who passed back and forth across borders, smuggling arms, equipment, people, and letters, at great risk to themselves. Once in Spain, someone would have posted the letter and then it would have taken its chances against German U-boats and bombers, as it crossed the Channel by ship.

'It seems impossible to imagine people crossing borders like that,' said Madeleine with a shudder. 'How brave! It's hard to believe people have the courage to regularly risk being caught.'

'Very brave,' agreed Isabelle. 'But when you believe in something so strongly, it drives you on.'

Hélène caught Flora's eye. The two women got on very well and together had assumed the role of protectors of Isabelle, trying to soften the blow of losing contact with James.

'Isabelle!' said Flora, who'd already guessed her friend's train of thought. 'Please tell me you're not considering what I think you're considering . . . '

'It could be done,' said Isabelle. 'I could travel to Spain, then find a courier to take me across the border into France. I'd just need papers — '

'Chérie! Non!' gasped Hélène staring

at her daughter with wild eyes. 'That's madness!'

Isabelle stood abruptly, running both hands through her hair, and glared at the three women.

'I can't think what else to do,' she said, her voice tinged with despair.

'Maman! Please don't go!' cried Madeleine as Isabelle strode out of the kitchen. 'Mémé, Flora! You won't let her go, will you?'

Hélène patted Madeleine's hand. 'Don't worry, Chérie, we'll think of something. It's probably the shock of that letter that's disturbed her, she's not thinking clearly. When she calms down, she'll realise it's a foolish idea.'

Despite Hélène's confident words, she held Flora's gaze and the two women silently conveyed their fear that Isabelle had been so low since they'd returned to England that she might be capable of any rash action.

17

Claude and Antoine had also escaped from the explosion of the storage depot with little more than cuts and bruises. After lying low for a week, they'd met with James and planned an attack on a German fuel store. New information and detonators had been received from London and a date set for a raid on the next moonless night.

The heavy clouds that had hung over the countryside on the day the sabotage was due to be carried out thickened as evening approached and descended as a light mist. It would be perfect for concealing the saboteurs from the German sentries, but unfortunately it also allowed the possibility that the resistance fighters might accidentally blunder into the guards.

Mathilde paced to and fro in her kitchen, dressed in her nightgown and clutching a cup of chicory coffee. She sipped at it distractedly without noticing it was cold.

Since her husband and son had died, she thought she'd lost the ability to care about anyone. She'd volunteered to help the Resistance, believing that her heart was no longer capable of feeling pain. But Luc, the Englishman who she knew was really called James, had somehow penetrated her shell. Had her son lived to reach Luc's age, she felt he would have been similar in disposition — brave, kind and loyal. Her son would have been a man that any mother would have been proud of — just like Luc.

As she paced the worn flagstones in the kitchen, she offered up a prayer for her husband and son, and a special one to keep Luc safe.

It was debatable whether her prayers had been answered — James had not died that night, but he hadn't escaped unscathed, being shot in the leg.

The fuel depot had been blown up in a spectacular explosion that Mathilde felt reverberate through the flagstones as she paced. The sky had lit up with a red glow that penetrated the fog and a heavy black cloud billowed upwards making the night even darker.

German soldiers were on the scene in minutes and no one knew if it had been due to luck or they had information about the planned sabotage. If they had arrived seconds earlier, the whole mission would have failed. It was hard to imagine that their appearance had been by chance.

Antoine and Claude managed to drag James away and help him back to Mathilde's farm house but he needed urgent medical attention. Claude brought a doctor to the house and he cleaned and bound James' wounds, but told him he needed more expert care than he could offer. He was sympathetic to the Resistance but the possibility of being caught giving medical assistance to one of its members obviously terrified him and he quickly left the farmhouse.

'Now what?' Mathilde asked.

'I believe there is a wounded British airman being flown out of France tomorrow night,' said Antoine. 'We must get them to take Luc home. There's nothing more we can do for him and he's lost a lot of blood. Thank God it's raining and washing the blood away or the German dogs would have traced us by now.'

'They may already know where we are,' said Claude gloomily. 'Dare we risk leading the Boches to the place where the British aircraft will land? If our group has been infiltrated, they may be waiting for us to make a move and lead them to another group.'

'Well, you can't leave him here,' said Mathilde. 'I'd willingly nurse him but he needs more care than I can give him, and we'll never be able to get him into the attic to hide him. If the Boches come now, they'll catch us all. If you think there's a chance you can get him home, you must take it.'

Claude nodded. 'I'll try to arrange something.'

* * *

James drifted in and out of consciousness, unaware of the panic around him. The doctor had left medicine to deaden the pain and Mathilde insisted on remaining with him to do whatever she could to make him as comfortable as possible.

The twin-engine Whitley was expected to land in a remote area about fifty kilometres from St-Pierre-sur-Somme. David Solomon, who had first arrived with James, had been killed during a raid on the railway and his replacement would be arriving with new radio equipment. A wounded RAF pilot would board the homeward bound plane with James. If all went well. There would be plenty of opportunity for things to go wrong.

During his lucid moments, James realised how worried Mathilde was

— Claude was convinced that their group had been betrayed to the enemy. The radio equipment that was being delivered was vital, and of course the wounded pilot would be needed by the RAF once he'd recovered. Carrying James home would add risk to an already fraught situation. If one of their Resistance group had betrayed them, then Mathilde would be in danger for having harboured him.

She insisted on accompanying him as they drove to the landing point, holding his head steady in her lap as the van jolted along rutted tracks. When they arrived, Antoine remained at the wheel while Claude met with the others who were waiting for the arrival of the British plane.

Mathilde tucked a piece of paper into James's pocket. On it was written Isabelle's name and address. If James was unconscious when he arrived in England, someone would find the paper and contact Isabelle. At least when he woke up, she would be there. Mathilde didn't allow herself to say *if* he woke up.

The Whitley was on time and the replacement operative and his radio equipment quickly disembarked, allowing the wounded pilot and James to be carried on. Within minutes, the engines were revving and the plane had started to taxi across the bumpy field.

There had been no time for good-byes, although Mathilde had held James's hand until the last moment and given it a squeeze as she let go and he was conveyed on to the plane.

One day, James thought, he would come back and thank Mathilde, Antoine and Claude — he owed them his life — but especially Mathilde. She had given him medication to deaden the pain on his journey and he knew his mind was beginning to drift, but a round of rapid gunfire brought him back to reality with a lurch. Claude had been right! One of their number had betrayed them. James felt sick, praying for a miracle for his friends.

Machine gun fire followed them as they rose into the air and the pilot veered sharply, trying to evade the attack. James was thrown against the side of the fuselage and remembered nothing more . . .

18

Madeleine checked the post each morning looking for letters from Spain — or anywhere else. For a while, she feared her mother would try to make her way to Spain despite Flora and Mémé's attempts to dissuade her. It was heart-breaking to see Isabelle so down and not for the first time, Madeleine silently cursed the man who seemed to have broken her mother's heart.

There were only two letters that morning. One, Madeleine knew, was from a regular client, but the other was from Hastings, Sussex. She eyed it with suspicion, turning it over in her hand as if, by handling it, its source might suddenly become apparent. But they knew nobody from that area.

She handed it to Isabelle silently, and prayed it wouldn't be more news about

James Hart, the man who'd cast a shadow over their lives. She saw her mother hesitate before slitting the envelope, taking out the letter and reading it.

The colour drained from Isabelle's face.

'What is it, Chérie?' Hélène asked.

'It's James! He was wounded in France and now he's in a hospital near Hastings!'

'How do you know?'

'The ward sister has written. She's asked if I'm able to go.'

No one asked if Isabelle was going. There was no question that she would rush to James's side.

'I'll come with you,' said Flora. 'We're not busy at the moment and you may need support.'

'Do you know what you're likely to find once you get there?' Hélène asked, and Isabelle passed the letter to her.

'He was shot while on some sort of mission in France, but on his way to England the plane was hit by enemy fire and although it made it back, it crash-landed and James hasn't regained consciousness. Apparently my name and address were in his pocket and the sister was hoping the sound of my voice might help his recovery . . . '

Isabelle faltered, and the tears she had been suppressing hovered on her lower lids.

'Right,' said Flora, taking a slice of toast from her plate and standing up. 'The sooner we get to Hastings and find out how he is, the better.'

Isabelle followed Flora upstairs to get dressed.

'What d'you think, Mémé?' Madeleine asked with a sigh, pushing her slice of toast round the plate with one finger.

'I have no idea, Chérie. All we can do is pray he's not too badly wounded . . . that he's not involved with that woman, Mathilde and no longer wants to know your mother . . . that he hasn't already recovered and gone back to France . . . or any other complications I haven't thought of. That's a lot of things to ask the Almighty for.'

Hélène and Madeleine stood at the door of Maison Maréchal watching Isabelle and Flora walk down the High Street towards Laindon Station. It was still early and both women wore thick coats, their gas mask containers slung across one shoulder bobbing against their hips as they walked at a fast pace. In Isabelle's hand, Madeleine could make out a handkerchief which her mother periodically held to her face. Hélène had spotted it too and both women knew Isabelle was wiping away tears.

'How could one man have upset Maman so?' Madeleine asked angrily as she turned away.

Hélène sighed. 'You wouldn't be so cross if you'd seen, how happy he made her, Chérie. We must hope they find each other again because it's going to take your maman some time to get over him if he dies . . . or doesn't want her.'

★ ★ ★

Flora hadn't intruded on Isabelle's thoughts during the train journey to Hastings. It had been a relatively easy trip and Isabelle spent most of the time staring out of the train window, although Flora was sure she hadn't taken in any of the countryside. She recognised the numbness that filled her friend, remembering how she'd felt when she'd been searching for her fiancé, Peter, in France. Her stomach was knotted with fear for her friend. What if there had been some mistake and it wasn't James at all? After all, the fact that a man had a scrap of paper with Isabelle's name on it in his pocket proved nothing. All she could do was to be there for Isabelle if she needed her.

'I'll wait here for you,' she said when they reached a tea shop. She gave Isabelle a hug. 'I'll be praying all is well.'

Isabelle returned the hug and carried

on along the road to St Margaret's Hospital.

★ ★ ★

The matron greeted Isabelle warmly and led her into an office.

'Please sit down, Mrs Maréchal. I'd like to have a chat with you before we go to the ward. Unfortunately, Lieutenant Hart has not yet regained consciousness. We believe he suffered trauma to his head in the plane that brought him back to England, and he'd lost a lot of blood from bullet wounds in his leg, so he is critically ill. Do you mind if I ask you if you know Lieutenant Hart well? We assumed that since your address was in his pocket, you were someone special to him. Are you family or friend?'

'Friend . . . very good friends.'

'Excellent. Then hopefully, the sound of your voice may get through to him and help his recovery. Shall we go?'

The smell of carbolic soap filled

Isabelle's nose as she followed Matron along the corridor to Harrison Ward. She hesitated at the door, afraid of what she was about to see and aware that these next few moments would determine her future — for better or worse.

Matron turned to check she was following and when she saw Isabelle standing uncertainly at the entrance to the ward, she smiled encouragingly.

'This way, Mrs Maréchal,' she said with a sympathetic smile.

Isabelle took a deep breath and followed her to the bed at the far end of the ward. With a start, she realised she could easily have walked past James without recognising him because of the extensive bruising on his face. His eyes were swollen and closed and he was motionless; only the rhythmic rise and fall of his chest revealed he was still alive.

'Are you all right, Mrs Maréchal?' Matron asked, taking her arm as she swayed. 'Here, take a seat and I'll get a nurse to bring you a glass of water.' She pulled a chair closer to James's bed and indicated she should sit.

'If you talk to him, Mrs Maréchal, it might bring him round. Just chatter about anything. You never know, it may help bring him back to us.'

Isabelle sat next to the bed and wondered what to say. She longed to touch him but the only part of him not covered by bed clothes was his face and she didn't want to hurt him. The starched sheets were tucked in and she dared not remove them to find his hand.

'James . . . ' she said wondering what to say to him. 'James, it's Isabelle. I . . . I . . . '

The man in the next bed saw her struggling for words. 'Why not tell him what happened to you after the last time you saw him, love?' he suggested. 'If that were me in that bed and my missus came to see me I'd probably want to know what 'appened after I'd last set eyes on her.'

Isabelle thanked him and started to

tell James about how she and Hélène had packed up all the things in the château, hoping each day to receive the telegram that never came, and how they'd returned to England and how she'd waited for him to send word, even though he had no idea where she was.

Visiting hours were over before she'd finished telling him about her new home and life.

'I'll come back later,' she whispered, leaning close to his face and very gently kissed him.

Suddenly, his eyes opened.

19

It was dark. It was warm. It should have been comfortable but it wasn't. There was a lot of pain. Sometimes, he thought he heard sounds coming from far away — echoing, haunting sounds — but when he focused on them, they turned into the shocking clash of bullets on metal. When he heard the gunfire an image always appeared in his mind of a woman's face but before he could study it and work out who she was, it dissolved.

This was very disturbing because he knew she was in danger and he wanted to help her but for some reason, his arms and legs wouldn't respond. And then it was silent and dark and warm again. One word spontaneously arose in his mind and he had the feeling it was the last word he'd uttered before he'd retreated into this black, lonely world . . . *Mathilde*.

Sometimes, it seemed like he'd been part of this blackness forever, but at others it was as if brightness and people were very near — close enough to reach out and touch. He just couldn't seem to summon the energy to do it.

Then he heard her calling. He recognised the voice, but who was she? Perhaps he'd open his eyes and find out.

The brightness seared his eyes but now he'd opened them, he refused to slip back into the darkness again and he fought to keep his eyelids open. Her face was close — so close, he could feel her breath on his cheek — and he wondered if this was the face that appeared when he heard gunfire. But she was too close to see clearly and his sight was blurred with tears that had flooded his eyes as they tried to adjust to the glare.

'Mathilde?' he asked hesitantly.

She instantly drew back then and he'd seen the pain register on her face.

'No, I'm Isabelle . . . '

Isabelle? He felt sure he should have known who she was but she was eluding him. It was like walking along a road . . . he knew there was something waiting for him around the corner but it wasn't there when he reached the bend . . . he knew it was now round the next corner . . . and then the next. Whatever was waiting was always out of reach.

'Lieutenant Hart.' It was a nurse standing next to the woman who'd called herself Isabelle, 'I'm just going to check your pulse and take your temperature, lie back and relax.'

The nurse had spoken to him soothingly and he was glad to be out of the dark, silent world where he'd been hiding but something was wrong.

What was it? The nurse had called him Lieutenant Hart. It didn't sound right. Perhaps she'd muddled him with someone else.

What was his name?

He had no idea.

20

Flora rose and rushed through the crowded tables towards Isabelle and led her back to where she'd been sitting waiting.

'What happened, Izzy? Wasn't it James?'

Isabelle's bottom lip trembled, 'It was him.'

'Is he in a state? Is he still unconscious?'

'No, he woke up while I was there . . . '

'But that's good, isn't it?'

Isabelle nodded. 'But he's lost his memory. He didn't remember me. He couldn't even remember who he was.'

'What did the doctors say, Izzy? It'll take time for his memory to return. At least he's home.'

'I'm not sure I want him to get his memory back,' Isabelle said.

'Whatever do you mean? Once he remembers everything, you'll have a second chance.'

'There was only one name he remembered and that was Mathilde. Whoever she is, she obviously made an impression on him. More than I did.'

'Oh, I see . . . What are you going to do?' Flora placed her hand over Isabelle's.

'I don't know,' Isabelle said, shaking her head sadly. 'Matron said I should go back at visiting time this afternoon. It may be he'll remember more during the day.'

Flora arranged for a cab to take them to Hastings and insisted they stroll along the front, taking in the sea breeze, and then find a small restaurant for lunch. She chattered about a dress she was making for Mrs Richardson at Priory Hall. Rationing had severely curtailed their business but they had adapted and had gained new customers who brought in old garments or curtains and asked for them to be made into something new. Mrs Richardson, however, seemed to be able to acquire new or barely used fabric to be made into beautiful outfits — although no one could say where she got the fabric from.

'Madeleine and Joanna seem so close. It's lovely that Maddie has such a good friend. I used to worry about her just having us in Guildford and not having any friends of her own. She dotes on Faye, too. I know Faye would love to help out more in the shop although I'm not sure Mrs Richardson would be happy about her granddaughter being a shop assistant! Joanna's son, Mark, is adorable too. He's so polite, such a little gentleman!'

Isabelle knew what Flora was doing and appreciated her efforts to keep her mind off James. She put her arm through Flora's as they walked past the fishermen's huts. Yes, it was wonderful that Madeleine had such a good friend in Joanna and Flora.

On the shingle beach, a man sat in

front of an easel, his loosely fitting smock billowing in the breeze. In his left hand, he held a palette and with his other, he dabbed at the canvas on the easel, one eye on the tall huts in which the fishermen stored their nets, and the other on his painting.

How peaceful, Isabelle thought. The artist looked as if he was so absorbed in painting, he wasn't aware of anything — not the wind whipping his smock, not the group of people standing behind him watching the picture materialise, not even the dog that threatened to shake its soaking coat nearby.

She suddenly remembered James's expression when he was sketching, as though his mind was elsewhere. She carried the sketches he'd done of her in her bag and she slipped her hand into it now to locate them and try to connect with the James she'd known.

How tragic that a man with a photographic memory now remembered nothing!

She recalled how he'd travelled to the Somme to find peace and to erase the horrors of the Great War, and now he wouldn't even remember that — nor this dreadful war either. But if sketching had helped him order his thoughts, might it be a way to unlock his memory now?

She checked her watch.

'It's time to find a cab back to the hospital,' she said, her voice stronger.

What would she do if he remembered and he'd made a new life with Mathilde and didn't want her? Then at least she will know. It would be time to move on and concentrate on Hélène, Madeleine and Flora. Although it would be painful, at last she'd know the truth and would be able to start afresh. It was time to leave the past behind.

* * *

For the second time that day, Isabelle entered the hospital and walked along the corridor to Harrison Ward. Nurses in starched uniforms and sensible shoes pushed men in wheelchairs and helped others walk along the corridor and out to the garden to sit in the sunshine.

When she arrived at James's bed, his eyes were closed, but as she sat down, he awoke.

He looked at her uncertainly.

'Hello,' she said as evenly as she could, 'I know you don't remember me but my name is Isabelle Maréchal and you and I met in France. At one time, we knew each other well.'

'I'm so sorry, Isabelle,' he said, frowning slightly. 'This must be very hard for you but I'm afraid I don't know you at all. There's only one name I remember and that's Mathilde. You don't know who she is, do you?'

Isabelle swallowed hard, 'No, I'm afraid not.'

He looked over her shoulder out of the window as if trying to recall who Mathilde was.

'I have some drawings you did,' she said. 'I wondered if they might spark some memories.' Isabelle took them out of her handbag and smoothed them out on the bed for him to see.

He frowned again as if trying to place the drawings, then looked up at her face.

'I didn't even know I could sketch,' he said sadly and winced as he moved his hand to mimic holding a pencil. 'But it feels as if I might be able to draw. It feels right, somehow.'

'When I come again, I'll bring a drawing pad and pencils,' she said.

'You'll come again? Though I don't know you?'

'Of course. You forget, I know you, even if you don't know me.'

*   *   *

Isabelle returned home that evening with Flora, then the following day — after packing a small suitcase and purchasing a sketch book and pencils at the station — she returned to Hastings and booked into a boarding house.

She would review her position at the end of the week and if there had been no progress, she'd think carefully about whether to stay or go home.

21

The woman who'd introduced herself as Isabelle returned the following morning. James hadn't expected her to come back. Exactly where she fitted into his past, he had no idea and he realised that other than saying they'd been friends, she hadn't said how close they'd been.

She was remarkably attractive and if there had been any interest on his part, it was completely understandable. In fact, 'remarkably attractive' was an understatement; she was bewitching.

The drawing of her by a river stirred something inside him but each time his mind reached out to seize it, the memory melted away. If only he could remember who Mathilde was. He had the feeling she was someone important and that she might be in danger. Before he allowed himself to indulge in thoughts of Isabelle and what had or had not been, he had to focus on Mathilde.

Isabelle brought him a sketch book and pencils and seemed disappointed when he placed them on the bedside table unopened. He thanked her but said that perhaps he'd try later.

She told him about her home in a small town called Montplessis, describing the château her mother owned, and Madame Picard who worked there. But other than a few moments when he thought memories might be coming back, she might as well have been describing somewhere he'd never visited.

He had very little to say, and yet Isabelle returned twice each day. Almost a week after she'd started coming, the nurses got James up and by the time she arrived, he was sitting in a wheelchair with a blanket over his legs in the garden. The nurses told him he was progressing well and would soon be able to go out to the garden on crutches. For the first time, he felt as if his life might be getting back on track.

Isabelle joined him under a large oak tree and he asked her to tell him about the sketch of her by the river. She blushed and lowered her gaze.

'We went to Beauvais to find a timber supplier for the château's roof. On the way back, we stopped off at the river,' she said.

'And that's it?' he asked disappointed.

'A Labrador ran up to us,' she added. 'And its owner called it back. Then we went home. Why do you ask? Do you remember something about it?'

'No, not really . . . it's just the way I drew you. Your mouth seems to be . . . '

'Yes?' Her eyes were willing him to remember.

'You look as though you're waiting for . . . ' he said, then, 'Perhaps I'm wrong.'

She sighed and looked down. 'Have you had any thoughts who Mathilde might be?' He shook his head sadly.

'Would it help to draw her?'

He hadn't thought of that. Perhaps if he stopped trying to remember and just drew, he might manage something that would give him a clue. After Isabelle left each evening, he'd started to sketch again. He'd drawn the nurses and matron from memory and after a few tries, his results had been quite pleasing, although he hadn't shown anyone.

'Shall I fetch your pad?' Isabelle asked.

'If you don't mind me drawing while you're here,' he said.

'I love to watch you draw,' she said and from the way she spoke, he knew she had watched him before and that they had definitely been more than friends, despite the details she left out.

He closed his eyes, and concentrating on the name Mathilde, he drew a few strokes, then looking at what he'd drawn. He shook his head.

'It might take time,' she said when she saw his disappointment.

'I suppose so. After all, this time last week, I wasn't even well enough to sit in a wheelchair in the garden. Who knows what progress I'll make? When you come in tomorrow ... ' He stopped when he saw her expression.

'I ... I probably won't be here tomorrow,' she said. 'I have to go home.'

'Oh.' He sagged slightly in the wheelchair. 'Of course.' His chest tightened at the thought of not seeing her. 'Yes, of course you have to go home.'

He sat drinking in the sight of her — the dappled sunlight making the highlights in her hair shine like copper strands, long lashes framing sensitive eyes, the upturned corners of her mouth. A mouth he could almost taste, lips he could almost feel against his ... Surely, they'd kissed in the past?

The sensations were too real to be imagination or wishful thinking. He forced the mental image of holding her in his arms away.

Think of Mathilde, he ordered himself. He'd inspected his ring finger for evidence that he'd ever worn a wedding ring but there was none. But that didn't mean he wasn't married or committed. And until he could remember, he dared not take any interest in anyone else.

Squaring his shoulders, he said in a firm voice, 'Yes, it's best you go home.'

When he saw the pain reflected in her eyes, he almost begged her to stay but it would have been unfair to express feelings he had no idea he had the right to possess. Feigning tiredness, he asked if she'd push his wheelchair back to the ward, hoping she would then leave. It was becoming agonising to be close to her and not know if he could offer her anything.

As she turned away, he caught sight of the tears welling in her eyes but she walked away with her back erect and strong. A groan escaped from his mouth, barely audible, but the man in the next bed obviously heard it.

'You're a fool, mate!' he said, 'Fancy lettin' a woman like that go! She's obviously mad about you — and you're mad about her.'

'It's not as simple as that, Ted,' James said and explained about Mathilde.

'Mathilde!' the man scoffed. 'It might be a dog for all you know!'

'No, I know it's a woman.'

'So what? I know you've got memory problems, mate, and I sympathise but there's a war on, and during a war, the rules change. You look about the same age as me, so I'm guessin' you fought in the last war as well?' James nodded. 'Yeah, I thought so. In that case you ought to know how fragile life is. It'd only take one Luftwaffe bomb on this hospital and we'd all be history. Don't let a chance at happiness slip through your fingers.'

'Look, Ted, I can't start something with Isabelle without knowing who Mathilde is. It's not fair.'

'Was it fair to break Isabelle's heart? I saw the tears as she walked away.'

'You might think 'love them and leave them' is a good way to behave, but — '

'No mate, during a war there's no time to love 'em and leave 'em — but you just left Isabelle. And you've left Mathilde too.'

22

James knew Isabelle had gone home but he couldn't help keeping an eye on the ward entrance during visiting hours just in case.

Several weeks after she'd left, he had a visitor from the Special Operations Executive. A tall, distinguished man dressed in a civilian suit carrying an attaché case — obviously of some importance, as Matron herself brought him in.

'Major Turnbull to see you, Lieutenant,' she said setting a chair next to the bed and pulling the curtains around them.

The major sat down.

'Matron tells me your memory has started to return,' he said. 'There wasn't much point coming to see you before, but rest assured, we've been keeping tabs on you. We like to keep an eye on our own.'

'Your own, Sir?'

'Ah,' said the major with a frown, 'You haven't yet remembered you were an SOE operative?'

'Well, that explains what I was doing in France for so long. I have brief memories of people and places but I'm struggling to remember names.'

Major Turnbull rested his attaché case on his lap and, raising the lid, extracted several sheets of paper and passed them to James.

'These should fill you in on your training and where you've been since 1941,' he said and leaned back while James read.

'That's helped a lot, Sir. Every day memories come back but they're like jigsaw puzzle pieces that don't fit together. This makes sense of quite a few things, but it doesn't cover what happened on my last assignment. It says we were targeting a German fuel depot and that it was destroyed, but not what happened after.'

'We were rather hoping *you'd* fill in the blanks there. The network seems to have been infiltrated and stopped operations but we don't know exactly what happened. It would be jolly useful if you remembered anything about it.'

James probed his memory using the information he'd just learned, but although fragments of the events leading up to and after the explosion appeared, he couldn't string them together.

'I remember two men . . . '

'Would they be Antoine Valluy and Claude Boutet?' Major Turnbull asked.

'Yes! Yes! That's right,' said James excitedly, 'Yes, they helped me back to the safe house and . . . ' He paused again as he fought to focus on the memory. 'I think it was Claude who was convinced our group had been betrayed. He was worried we would lead the Germans to the landing place and endanger the other group who were waiting for an agent and radio equipment. I think a wounded pilot was also being flown home.'

'The pilot recovered but couldn't tell us anything about why you were on the flight, other than the plane came under attack as it took off.'

'Do you know if Claude, Antoine and Mathilde,' — the name was out of his mouth before he realised. 'Mathilde! That's who she is!' James explained to Major Turnbull how he'd remembered the name and felt she was in danger but couldn't remember who she was until that moment.

'Do we know what happened to them? Did the Germans get them?'

'As far as I know, Claude Boutet is alive and has joined another group. I'm afraid Antoine was shot that evening and later died. As for Mathilde, I don't know but I'll certainly try to find out.'

Major Turnbull checked his watch, 'Well, I have a train to catch, so I'll leave now. If anything else occurs to you, please write it down, Lieutenant. I'll be back next week to check your progress.'

He stood up, tucked the attaché case under his arm, pulled the curtains aside and left.

James lay back on the pillows, exhausted with the effort of remembering, but at least now he knew who Mathilde was. He rummaged in the bedside table for the sketch pad Isabelle had left him. Closing his eyes, he brought Mathilde's face into his mind's eye ... like photographic paper in a developing tray ... first blank, then gradually shadows and highlights forming indistinct features which gradually sharpened until he could see her face clearly. He began to draw.

'What've you been drawing?' Ted asked when James put his pencil down and leaned back.

James turned the sketch pad so Ted could see, 'It's Mathilde,' he said. 'I've finally remembered.'

'Blimey, she looks like your mother! I was expecting some fancy French girlie!'

As far as James could remember, it was an accurate likeness of Mathilde's features. She'd always made sure he had enough to eat from the meagre supplies, even pretending she'd no appetite so he would have sufficient. He looked at the wrinkles around her eyes, the worry lines on her forehead and remembered the kindness born from the pain of losing her husband and son. No wonder her name had been uppermost in his mind when she'd put herself in danger on that last journey to the landing site.

'So, you gonna find your Isabelle now you know who the mysterious Mathilde is?' Ted asked.

'I'm not sure she'll want to know. She said she'd come back but she hasn't. Perhaps she doesn't want a life with a crippled amnesiac.'

'Rubbish!' said Ted. 'You're remembering stuff every day and you're up on crutches now. You'll walk out of here on your own two legs, mark my words. What're you waiting for?'

★　★　★

Ted usually took a stroll round the corridors before bedtime. He'd been shot in the shoulder and much of the bone had been shattered, but he was still mobile and liked to walk about just because he could. On his way past Matron's office, he knocked and waited until she called him in.

'Private Sterling, you should be in bed. You know I don't approve of you wandering about.'

'It keeps me sane, Matron. Anyway, I'll be quick and then get back to bed. It's Lieutenant Hart, he's pining for that lady what came to see him and I wondered if you could do anything about it.'

'It's not up to me, I'm afraid. I wrote to her to let her know he was here but she hasn't returned.'

'No, but she should. Can't you write again?'

'Lieutenant Hart could write if he wanted to.'

'He's not got her address. D'you still have it?'

'Possibly,' she said rising and pulling out a large drawer. She rifled through the contents and pulled out a slip of paper, 'Yes, this is it.'

'Can I take it to him?'

'I suppose so,' said Matron. 'So long as you go straight back to bed and mind that arm. I'll get Nurse Isaac to re-do that sling.'

Ted took the slip of paper and whistled his way back to his bed.

23

Madeleine's heart sank. There was only one letter in the post that morning. It was for her mother and it was from Hastings. Maman had been happier since she'd returned from her week in Sussex visiting that man. Well, not happier, but settled — resigned would be a better description. At least the despair that haunted her since she'd returned with Mémé from France had gone.

At last Madeleine could see that, in time, things would get back to normal. But now with this letter from Hastings, who could say what would happen? Was it from James Hart? Madeleine turned the letter over but there was no clue. The handwriting appeared to be a man's but appearances could be deceptive. It crossed her mind to steam it open but was too afraid of being caught. Suppose she simply threw it away?

Perhaps she'd ask Flora what to do. Until then, she'd tuck it in the hall table drawer. Before she could get Flora on her own, there was a knock at the door. It was Joanna with Faye who was holding a tiny puppy nestled in her arms.

'Look, Maddie, look! It's my new puppy! Isn't he adorable? I'm going to call him Pipkin. What d'you think, Maddie? Don't you just love him?'

It was several days before the letter was discovered in the hall drawer.

★　★　★

'Oh, Maman, I'm so sorry,' Madeleine said when the letter finally found its way to Isabelle. 'Faye came with Pipkin and I forgot. And to tell you the truth, I . . . I . . . wasn't sure about giving it to you and risking upsetting you.'

'I understand,' said Isabelle. It wasn't James's writing — she knew that.

Neither was it Matron's. She was tempted to throw it away unopened but knew she'd always wonder who had written. She took a deep breath and opened the letter . . .

Dear Isabelle,

I don't suppose you'll remember me but my name is Ted Sterling, in the bed next to James Hart in Harrison Ward. I wonder if you're free to visit? I know James will be pleased to see you.

Yours sincerely,

Edward Sterling

Isabelle stared at the letter, She remembered the pleasant man in the bed next to James, who had encouraged her to speak to James when he was still unconscious, but it was a puzzle why James hadn't written himself if he was so keen to see her. She passed the letter to Hélène, Flora and Madeleine. The three women sat silently waiting for Isabelle to say something.

Finally, Hélène spoke, 'Will you go, Chérie?'

'I'll always wonder if I don't, but — '

Madeleine stood with such force her chair tipped over backwards.

'Why doesn't that man leave you alone, Maman? Ever since you met him he's torn you apart. And he's torn us apart too! Why can't he just go away?'

She rushed from the room and Isabelle stood to follow her.

'Leave her, Chérie,' said Hélène. 'She's worried for you, that's all. if she'd seen how happy you were with James, she wouldn't have said that. Now, why don't you get your coat and go now? You need to know where you stand.'

24

When Hélène again suggested that she go to Hastings and find out what had happened to make Ted write, Isabelle said, 'No, Maman, Madeleine must be my first concern.'

'She's just worried about you, Chérie. She didn't mean it.'

'No, it's time to admit the truth to myself. I have you, Flora and our beautiful Madeleine — that's enough. I loved once, that's more than some people ever have. It's time to think of the future and forget the past. If this war ever ends, I want to go back to France, and renovate the château. That's what I'm going to focus on now.'

Hélène shook her head sadly but said no more. It was obvious Isabelle had given her decision much thought and it wasn't as though Ted's letter offered any hope — it had simply said he knew

James would be pleased to see her. Perhaps he was wrong — kind and thoughtful, but wrong.

Later, she took Madeleine aside and told her that Isabelle had decided to ignore the letter.

'I only want Maman to be happy,' she said. 'I don't think I helped though, did I?'

'It's hard to say, Chérie. It looks as though the fates are against them. Perhaps your maman is doing the sensible thing. Only time will tell.'

★ ★ ★

Madeleine was quiet for the rest of the day, puzzling over Ted's letter, wondering what James was like. After work, she walked to Joanna's house and told her everything.

'So, what would you do? You're the only woman I know who's happy in love. If you were my mother, would you go to Hastings?'

'It doesn't really matter what I'd do,

317

Maddie. But it sounds like your mother's made up her mind to move on. That takes strength.'

'But I can't help feeling that if I hadn't said anything, she'd have gone to see him . . .'

'I don't suppose you'll ever know.'

Madeleine sighed and tickled Pipkin's ears. He licked her hand and nudged it so it was positioned over his ear again and looked at her hopefully.

'I could find out . . .' she said slowly.

'How? Oh, no, Maddie, please tell me you're not going to do what I think you're going to do!'

'If I don't go and see him, I'll never know.'

'I really don't think you should interfere.'

'Too late, I've already interfered. I don't think I can make it worse.'

'But suppose he's remembered he's married to the mysterious Mathilde? Would your mother want to know that? You might make things worse.'

'Not if she doesn't know.'

318

The following Saturday, Madeleine announced she was going to spend the day with Joanna. She set off on her bicycle towards Joanna's house, but instead, stopped at Laindon Station and bought a ticket to Hastings . . .

25

James was sitting in the hospital garden. He'd made the short distance from his bed, down the corridor, and across the lawn to the bench using just a cane. Although he'd always limp, in time he'd be able to walk without aid. Not only that, he would soon be discharged from hospital.

The thought filled him with excitement — and dread. Ted had been discharged a few days earlier and had given James the slip of paper with Isabelle's address. He deliberately hadn't thought about where he'd go, hadn't thought about the future much at all. He wanted to find Isabelle but knew he shouldn't . . .

He looked up, and for a second, wondered if he was dreaming. There at the door was Isabelle with a nurse pointing towards him. She stepped into the garden but as she walked towards him, bitter disappointment washed over him. This woman was much younger than Isabelle — she had chestnut curls, not long hair, but she tipped her head to one side the same way as Isabelle.

'Hello,' she said holding out her hand. 'I'm Madeleine, Isabelle's daughter. I've come to . . . well, I don't know what I've come to do. Apologise . . . explain . . . I rehearsed what to say all the way on the train but the truth is, it all depends on you really . . . '

★　★　★

Madeleine hurried back to the railway station. She dared not be late in case her mother discovered where she'd been and was upset. She was pleased she'd visited James — he'd surprised her. She'd always thought of him as a problem, an obstacle to Maman's happiness, but he wasn't like that at all and if he could make Maman happy . . .

The large, flat parcel tied with string lay waiting for Isabelle the following morning. Flora and Hélène had finished breakfast early and gone to London to buy fabric. Isabelle sat down at the table and turned the parcel over.

'Where did this come from? There's no stamp.'

'It was hand-delivered,' Madeleine said, avoiding her mother's gaze.

Isabelle cut the string and peeled off the brown paper. Inside was a sketch pad. She lifted the cover to reveal a portrait of a thin woman with weather-beaten skin. Although the woman was smiling, there was sadness in her eyes and it was easy to imagine her life had been a hard one.

Isabelle recognised the style. She knew without looking at the signature at the bottom that the artist was James. Beneath the face was written *Mathilde Deloffre, member of the French Resistance (1888-1942) Killed in action.*

May she rest in peace with her husband and son.

Isabelle stared at the strong face. This woman had made an impression on James — but not as she'd once feared.

Isabelle turned to the next page and caught her breath. It was a drawing of her . . . as was the next . . . and the next . . . one after another, in various settings, others with no setting at all, but in each picture, she looked out of the page eagerly, her lips open as if about to receive a kiss and with love shining in her eyes at the beholder.

That's how he sees me in his imagination, she realised with a thrill.

'I'm just off to Joanna's before I open the shop. Mémé and Flora will be back at five. By the way, the person who delivered the parcel is waiting for a reply . . . ' Madeleine said, adding, ' . . . at the front door.'

Isabelle flew to the door, pulling it open with a wild jangling of the bell and stepped out onto the street. A man with a walking cane and small suitcase was waiting.

'I've remembered everything,' he said. 'Well, I think I've remembered everything and I've drawn what I can recall.'

'You don't have much eye for fashion, do you? I seem to have bare shoulders much of the time. Although the flower in my hair was a nice touch. And you remembered my pearl hair combs . . . '

'Hmm, my imagination ran away with me a little, but I thought I handled the subject very tastefully. Do you mind?'

'No, but I was surprised to see so many drawings. I thought you'd lost interest in me.'

'Once my memory started to come back, I realised how much I love you.'

'But why didn't you contact me back before we left France?'

James explained about how Mathilde had discovered that Monsieur Charbonel had intercepted his telegrams and destroyed them.

'Hideous, hateful man!' exclaimed Isabelle.

'Sadly, he paid the price for his dishonesty. Someone left him in a burned-out car in a ditch.'

'Oh! He didn't deserve that . . . '

'You don't always get what you deserve,' James said with a sigh. 'We didn't deserve to be torn apart. Fate hasn't been kind to us, has it? The question is, can we recover anything?' He put his arms round her waist and pulled her close, looking into her eyes, 'Can we?'

'It's hard to say.' She stood on tiptoe and brushed his lips with hers, 'What do you think?'

As he cupped her face in his hands a look of disquiet passed over her face and she placed her hands over his.

'Will you meet my daughter, Madeleine? I wouldn't do anything to upset her and I've been so miserable since I came back to England without you, I'm afraid she blames you.'

'We have her blessing,' he said, smiling. 'She visited me yesterday and suggested I come. She's a wonderful young lady. But what would you expect with such a marvellous mother?'

'She visited you in hospital?' Isabelle gasped.

'She came yesterday and we had a long chat. I was able to assure her I had intended to join you in England and I hadn't simply abandoned you.'

It must be true. Isabelle thought back to when Madeleine had handed her the parcel earlier. She knew James was waiting for her outside.

'I spent the night wondering what to do and this morning, I discharged myself and here I am.'

'And what shall we do now?'

'Right now,' he said, 'I think we do this . . . '

His mouth sought hers and kissed her hungrily. She pressed against him, feeling her body mould to his as if they had been sculpted to fit together.

A moment later, they pulled apart

abruptly at the sound of voices outside the front door.

'Ah, found them!' There was a clatter as a bunch of keys dropped to the pavement.

'For crying out loud! Can't you make a bit more noise? D'you want the world to know we're late?'

Isabelle disengaged herself from James and rushed to the door and opened it.

'Ooh! Madame Maréchal! I'm so sorry we're late, Molly couldn't find her keys and . . . '

'Never mind,' said Isabelle. 'Something unexpected has come up and we'll have to stay closed today, so you've got the day off.'

There was a pause as Isabelle's words sank in.

'Shoo!' she said waving her hands at them and they turned away, squealing with delight.

Isabelle locked the door, changed the sign on the door to *Closed* and moved back to James.

'That should ensure we're not disturbed for a while.' She put her arms round his neck and pulled him towards her.

'As tempting as it is to hold you in my arms until someone else disturbs us, I feel we need to discuss our future plans,' he said.

'Our future plans,' she echoed, savouring the words. 'What did you have in mind?'

'For a start, we'll never, ever be apart again — unless you.want to be rid of me, of course.'

She laid her cheek against his chest. 'Never.'

'It came to me I should start an architectural business. This war can't last for ever and people will want to rebuild. And one day, if it's possible to return to Montplessis, we could renovate Château Bellevais. By the way, did you see the final portrait in my sketchbook?'

'The one where I'm admiring a ring on my fourth finger?'

He nodded. 'How about we take a leaf out of that book and make it a reality?'

It had taken two wars, but they had found each other at last and would never be parted again.